OTHELLO

GOLD EDITION

WILLIAM SHAKESPEARE

ISBN: 979-8-8693-0822-1

CONTENTS

INTRODUCTION

Welcome to Adaptive Reader, your portal to the captivating world of literature, tailored to fit your unique reading abilities.

In today's fast-paced and diverse learning environment, we believe in the power of personalized learning experiences. That's where the concept of leveled reading comes in, and why we, at Adaptive Reader, have dedicated ourselves to offering a broad collection of classic novels at various reading levels. Our mission is to make the joy and benefits of reading accessible to everyone.

THE BENEFITS OF LEVELED TEXTS

So, what exactly is leveled reading? It's an approach that matches students with texts that align with their unique reading abilities. This ensures that every reader is challenged just the right amount - enough to grow, but not so much that they feel overwhelmed or frustrated.

For students, this means you'll engage with texts that stretch your reading skills while keeping the experience enjoyable and manageable. You'll gain confidence as you successfully comprehend each level and feel motivated to explore more challenging texts as your reading skills grow.

For teachers, Adaptive Reader provides a valuable tool to support differentiated instruction. You can assign the same novel to your entire class while ensuring each student reads a version that aligns with their reading level. This allows all students to participate in class discussions and activities, fostering a more inclusive learning environment.

For parents, Adaptive Reader offers a supportive tool to encourage your children's reading journey. As your child progresses through the different levels of a novel, they'll not only enhance their reading skills but also develop a deeper love for literature.

READING ACROSS MULTIPLE EDITIONS

All of our leveled novels include passage markers that correspond to the same content across every one of our editions. This means that passage '62' in our silver edition contains the same themes and plot elements as passage '62' in our original edition.

For teachers, this means that you can say "let's look at passage 35 together. What is the author trying to tell us here?" and all of your students will be reading the same content — but with vocabulary and syntax that's adapted to their reading level.

Our online reading tool, available at www.adaptivereader.com, gives students and teachers free access to the original text with passage markers. We encourage teachers to include close readings of the original text as part of their coursework, giving all students exposure to the rich original syntax and language of these exceptional authors.

THE POWER OF LITERATURE

At Adaptive Reader, we are committed to helping everyone experience the power of literature. So whether you're a student diving into a classic novel, a teacher looking for flexible resources, or a parent seeking ways to support your child's literacy, Adaptive Reader is here for you.

We invite you to embark on this exciting literary journey with us. Enjoy the world of stories, characters, and ideas that await you in our collection of leveled novels. Happy reading!

DRAMATIS PERSONÆ

DUKE OF VENICE: Duke of Venice.

BRABANTIO: Senator of Venice, Desdemona's father.

SENATORS: Duke's assistants.

GRATIANO: Brabantio's brother.

LODOVICO: Brabantio's relative.

OTHELLO: A Moor and a high-ranking official.

CASSIO: Othello's Lieutenant.

IAGO: Othello's Military Captain.

MONTANO: Governor of Cyprus prior to Othello.

RODERIGO: Gentleman of Venice.

CLOWN: Othello's servant.

DESDEMONA: Brabantio's daughter and Othello's wife.

EMILIA: Iago's wife.

BIANCA: Cassio's lover.

In addition, there are various officers, gentlemen, a messenger, musicians, a herald (messenger), a sailor, and servants.

SCENE: Act I is in Venice. Following acts are at a seaport in Cyprus.

ACT I

SCENE 1. VENICE. A STREET.

2   *[Enter Roderigo and Iago.]*

RODERIGO:

Hey, I'm not happy about this.

You, Iago, you've long controlled my finances so much.

It's like you thought my money was actually yours.

You should've told me.

IAGO:

Honestly, it's crazy that you won't listen to me.

If I ever even dreamed of such a thing, you would hate me.

RODERIGO:

You once told me that you don't even like him.

IAGO:

Indeed, it would be amazing if I didn't.

Three influential people in this city,

Personally asked me to be their lieutenant.

They even took off their hats! I'll tell you,

I know my own worth, I deserve at least that position.

But he, so in love with himself,
Avoids my requests.
He rejects those who support me and says,
"I've already selected my officer."
But who is this officer?
Well, it's a great mathematician,
Michael Cassio, from Florence.
A man almost ruined by his beautiful wife,
A man who has never led an army in the field,
A man who knows about real war
No more than a housemaid (unless reading about it counts).
It's all babble without any real experience!
That's all his soldiership is! But he got the job,
And I, whose skills he has seen with his own eyes,
In Rhodes, in Cyprus, and elsewhere,
Under both Christian and non-Christian banners,
I am being ignored, shrugged off
By this man who only knows how to count money!
When the time is right, he will become his lieutenant.
And me, I'm just his old faithful assistant.

RODERIGO:
Ugh. I rather wish to be his executioner.

IAGO:
Look, there's nothing we can do about it.
It's the drawback of serving others.
Promotion comes from favoritism and special connections,
Not by the old system where you earn promotions.

RODERIGO:
I wouldn't follow him.

IAGO:
Oh, my friend, just relax.
I only follow him to serve my own interests.
We can't all be leaders,
Just like not all leaders can truly be followed.

You'll see many a servant who, obsessed with his service,

Spends their time acting like a donkey working for his master.

He works for food and then is thrown away when he's old.

Those are the honest fools who deserve a whipping.

But there are others who

Keep their hearts focused on their own interests.

They only put on an act of service for their masters,

And in doing so, they thrive.

I'm one of them.

I promise you, if I were him, I wouldn't want to be me.

By following him, I'm really following my own interests.

My actions will display the true feelings of my heart.

I'll make my emotions known for birds to peck at.

Although, I am not what I appear to be.

RODERIGO:

Just think of the incredible luck the Moor has

if he can get away with this!

IAGO:

Here's the plan:

Wake up her father and turn his joy against him.

Make sure his relatives dislike him.

Even though he lives in a favorable environment,

Torture him. Make him miserable.

RODERIGO:

Here's her father's house.

I'll shout to get his attention.

IAGO:

Do it, and make your voice sound as frightened

And urgent as a person who's discovered a fire in a crowded city.

RODERIGO:

Hey there, Brabantio! Mr. Brabantio, hello!

IAGO:

Wake up Brabantio! Thieves, thieves!

Protect your house, your daughter,

And your belongings! Thieves, thieves!

Brabantio appears at an upstairs window.

BRABANTIO:

What's the meaning of this urgent call? What's going on?

RODERIGO:

Sir, is your entire family inside your house?

IAGO:

Have you locked your doors?

BRABANTIO:

Wait, why are you asking this?

IAGO:

My goodness, sir, you've been robbed!

For your own dignity, put on your robe.

Your heart is broken,

You've lost something precious.

At this moment, a black man is with your white daughter.

Get up, alert your fellow citizens with the sound of a bell.

Otherwise, you'll end up a grandfather

Before you even know it. Get up, I say!

BRABANTIO:

What, have you lost your minds?

RODERIGO:

Respected sir, do you recognize my voice?

BRABANTIO:

Not I. Who are you?

RODERIGO:

I am called Roderigo.

BRABANTIO:

That is not a welcome name.

I told you not to hang around my home.

I've told you before:

My daughter is not meant for you.

Now, in your foolish manner,

Full of dinner and strong drink,

You ruin my peace!
RODERIGO:
Respectfully, sir...
BRABANTIO:
You need to realize
My influence and my position have the power
To make this very unpleasant for you.
RODERIGO:
Patience, honorable sir.
BRABANTIO:
What do you mean by mentioning robbery?
This is Venice. My house is not a simple farm.
RODERIGO:
Respected Brabantio,
In innocence and sincerity, I come to you.
IAGO:
Sir, you seem one who wouldn't serve God
If the devil told you to.
We've come to help, but you see us as rough men.
Because of this, you'll find your daughter with a north-African horse.
You may have to endure horse-related jokes from your nephews...
BRABANTIO:
What kind of a strange intruder are you?
Speak plainly.
IAGO:
I am one, sir, who comes to tell you that,
Your daughter and Othello are together now.
BRABANTIO:
You are a villain.
IAGO:
You are a senator.
BRABANTIO:
You'll answer for this.

I recognize you, Roderigo.

RODERIGO:

Sir, I'm ready to respond. But I beg you,

Your lovely daughter,

At this strange and late time of night,

Was taken away with just a common servant, a gondolier,

To the lustful Moor.

If you know about this, and you let it happen,

Then we apologize for our disrespect.

However, if this is all new to you,

Then according to my manners,

We've received a telling off where it isn't needed.

I would never toy with your respect and authority.

Your daughter (if you haven't given her approval)

I'll say it again, has shamefully rebelled,

Binding her obligation, beauty, intelligence, and her wealth

To an unpredictable stranger

Who comes from here and everywhere.

Just go find out for yourself.

If your daughter is in her room or at your house now,

then let me take the blame from your government for tricking

you like this.

BRABANTIO:

Strike and make a fire, everyone!

Get me a torch! Gather all my people!

This is not different from my dream,

Believing in it is already getting me down.

Lights, I want lights!

Exit from above.

IAGO:

Goodbye. I have to leave you now.

It doesn't seem appropriate for my position

To stand out or make a scene while I'm here, because if I stay,

I'll have to fight the Moor. You see, I know that the government

Cannot just throw him away because he's

Set to lead the fight in the Cyprus wars.

These wars are about to start any minute now.

We don't have anyone else who's capable of leading the charge.

So even though I hate him as much as I hate the pains of hell,

To survive, I must not fight with him.

Sure enough, you'll find him there,

Go with a search party,

And I'll meet you there. So, goodbye.

Exit. Brabantio enters with servants and torches.

BRABANTIO:

It's a sad truth. She is indeed gone,

And all there is nothing but sorrow. Now Roderigo,

Where did you see her? (How could this happen to my dear daughter!)

With the Moor, you say? (What a father's sorrow!)

How did you know it was her? (I can't believe she tricked me

so badly.) What did she say to you? Light more torches,

Gather all of our family. Do you think they're married?

RODERIGO:

Yes, I think they might indeed be.

BRABANTIO:

Oh no! How did she even go? This is betrayal!

From now on, fathers, don't trust your daughter's actions!

Could she have been tricked?

Have you not heard of such stories, Roderigo?

RODERIGO:

Yes, sir, I have indeed.

BRABANTIO:

Get my brother.

We all try different paths. Do you know

Where we might find her and the Moor?

RODERIGO:

I think I know where he is, provided

You get good security and come with me.
BRABANTIO:
Please lead us. At every house I'll ask,
I have the power to do so. Get weapons, hurry!
And fetch some special night guards.
Lead us, Roderigo. I appreciate your efforts.

Exit.

SCENE 11. VENICE. ANOTHER STREET

8   *[Enter Othello, Iago and Attendants with torches.]*

IAGO:
Though I've killed men in the line of war,
I believe it's deeply important
To never plot murder. I lack the wickedness
To get things done, but I felt like stabbing him.
OTHELLO:
It's better the way it is.
IAGO:
Well, but with the way he was talking,
Saying such terrible things about you,
I barely restrained myself from him. But I ask you, sir,
Are you securely married? Be sure of this,
There's a lot of love from the people
And his influence has a powerful voice
Twice as strong as the duke's. He will try to separate you,
Or impose upon you any restriction

The law will allow him.

OTHELLO:

Let him do his worst.

My services, which I have performed for the senate,

Will speak louder than his complaints. It's still unknown—

But I see now that boasting is a sign of respect, so

I shall make it public — I owe my life and existence

To men of royal status. My worth

Can be openly praised to as proud a fortune

Just like the one I've achieved. You see, Iago,

If it were not for my love for the gentle Desdemona,

I would not let go of my freedom for all the treasure there is.

But look, who's coming there?

IAGO:

Her angry father and his allies.

You'd better go inside.

OTHELLO:

No, they must find me here.

My abilities, my respected position, and my spotless soul

Will show them who I am. Are they the ones?

IAGO:

I don't think so.

Enter Cassio and Officers carrying torches.

OTHELLO:

These are the duke's men and my deputy.

Good evening to you, friends!

Any news?

CASSIO:

The duke sends his greetings, general,

And he urgently requests

Your immediate presence.

OTHELLO:

What seems to be the matter?

CASSIO:

Something important from Cyprus, if I'm not mistaken.
This urgent business has sent a series of messengers
All throughout the night and many of the leaders,
Are already at the duke's. You have been eagerly looked for,
And when you couldn't be found at your house,
The senate has sent three different search parties
To find you.
OTHELLO:
Good that you found me.
I just need a moment in the house,
And I'll go with you.

Exit.

CASSIO:
What's he doing here?
IAGO:
Well, tonight he's gained something.
If it's legally his, he's set for life.
CASSIO:
I'm not following.
IAGO:
He's married.
CASSIO:
To whom?

Enter Othello.

IAGO:
Well, he's marrying—So, captain, are you coming?
OTHELLO:
I'll go with you.
CASSIO:
Here comes another group looking for you.
 Enter Brabantio, Roderigo and Officers carrying torches and weapons.
IAGO:
That's Brabantio. General, be alert,
He's angry.

OTHELLO:
Wait! Stop right there!
RODERIGO:
Signior, it's the Moor.
BRABANTIO:
Arrest him, thief!

Weapons are drawn on both sides.

IAGO:
You, Roderigo! Come on, I'm ready for you.
OTHELLO:
Put away your shiny swords,
They'll get rusty.
Dear Signior, you will have more control
With the passing of years
Than with your weapons.
BRABANTIO:
Oh, you disgusting thief, where have you hidden my daughter?
Curse you! You must have bewitched her.
I really question whether a girl so innocent, fair, and cheerful,
So against the idea of marriage that she
Ignored many suitors of our society,
Would ever decide to leave safety for the embrace
Of someone like you.
Let the world judge me if it's not clear.
You've tricked her with wicked spells,
Harmed her purity with potions or minerals
That have weakened her strength.
I'll demand an investigation!
I thus arrest and charge you
As a menace of the world, a practitioner
Of witchcraft.—
Arrest him! If he resists,
Handle him at your own risk!
OTHELLO:

Stand down!
If it were my time to battle, I would have known it
Without needing a reminder. Where do you want me to go
To answer these accusations?

BRABANTIO:
To jail, until it's time for court.

OTHELLO:
What if I simply agree to answer your questions?
One more thing. How is it possible that the duke feels satisfied,
When his representatives are here by my side,
With pressing business of the state,
To take me to him?

OFFICER:
Indeed, respected sir,
The duke's in a meeting. I'm sure
They have called for you as well.

BRABANTIO:
Really? The duke in a meeting?
At this hour in the night? Let's go then.
This matter of mine is not to be dismissed. The duke himself,
Or any of my fellow statesmen,
Can't help but feel this wrongdoing as if it were their own.
For if such deeds can go unpunished,
Then our politicians will be as bad as slaves and savages.

Everyone exits.

SCENE III. VENICE. A COUNCIL CHAMBER

12   *[Enter the Duke and Senators sit at a table. Officers are present.]*

DUKE:

I don't find these news reports believable.

FIRST SENATOR:

Indeed, they seem unrealistic.

My information counts a hundred and seven ships.

DUKE:

My source claims a hundred and forty.

SECOND SENATOR:

And I have information on two hundred ships.

Though these numbers don't entirely match,

They all confirm the existence of a very large

Turkish fleet of ships, heading toward Cyprus.

DUKE:

Well, such a thing is possible.

It's definitely cause for concern.

SAILOR:

[From offstage.] Hey! Hey! Hey!
OFFICER:

There's a messenger from the ships.

The Sailor enters.

DUKE:

Alright,—what's the urgent news?

SAILOR:

The Turkish forces are gathering strength at Rhodes,

That's the report I was told to deliver here.

DUKE:

What do you think of this development?

FIRST SENATOR:

This can't be logical. It's a distraction

To mislead us. When we take into account

The strategic importance of Cyprus to the Turks,

We may realize once more,

That if an attack is more likely to be on Cyprus than on Rhodes,

The Turks can manage it more easily.

Cyprus is not as protected,

It lacks the defensive advantages that Rhodes has.

If we consider this,

We can't underestimate the Turks' strategy.

It seems the less important issues he deals with last,

Ignoring an opportunity for ease and benefit,

To awaken and start a needless fight.

DUKE:

No, I'm fully confident, he's not aiming for Rhodes.

OFFICER:

We have more news.

Enter a Messenger.

MESSENGER:

The Ottoman Turks, respected and noble,

Plotting a direct course for the island of Rhodes,

Have joined with a secondary fleet there.

FIRST SENATOR:

Yes, I had guessed. How many do you estimate?

MESSENGER:

About thirty ships, and now they're turning

Their course around, openly revealing

Their plans towards Cyprus. Signior Montano,

Your reliable and brave servant,

Sends his greetings and asks you to trust him.

DUKE:

It's then confirmed, we're heading for Cyprus.

Is Marcus Luccicos not in town?

FIRST SENATOR:

He's currently in Florence.

DUKE:

Communicate with him at once. This is urgent.

FIRST SENATOR:

Arriving now are Brabantio and the brave Moor.

Enter Brabantio, Othello, Iago, Roderigo and Officers.

DUKE:

Brave Othello, we must immediately assign you

Against our common enemy, the Ottoman.

[To Brabantio.] I didn't see you. Welcome, honorable sir,

We missed your advice tonight.

BRABANTIO:

The feeling is mutual. Dear Duke, please excuse me.

Neither my role, nor anything about this business

Got me out of bed, nor does the problem

Interest me. My household grief is so overpowering

That it consumes all other sorrows.

And it is still itself.

DUKE:

Why, what's the matter?

BRABANTIO

My daughter! Oh, my daughter!
DUKE and **SENATORS**:
Dead?!
BRABANTIO:
To me, she might as well be.
She's taken, stolen from me, and changed
By trickery from tricksters.
It's against nature for her to behave like this.
She is not a senseless girl.
Without deception, it could not happen.
DUKE:
Whoever did this, who tricked your daughter,
And robbed you of her, will face punishment.
BRABANTIO:
I appreciate your support.
Here is the man, this stranger, whom it seems
you called here for political reasons.
ALL:
We're sorry.
DUKE:
[To Othello.] What's your story?
BRABANTIO:
I can add nothing, except that it's true.
OTHELLO:
Most powerful, honorable, and respected men,
My masters:
I confess, I've married her.
The extent of my wrongdoing
Is just this, no more. I may lack eloquence,
And don't have the skills for peaceful negotiation.
Since these arms were strong enough for battle,
Up until recently – some nine months prior,
They have only been used for fighting wars.
Therefore, my knowledge about the world of love is limited,

And only relates to conflict and combat.

And so, I won't do much in defending myself.

But with your patience,

I promise to tell the full story

Of my complete course of love: the potions, the enchantments,

And the powerful magic,

That I'm accused of using to win his daughter.

BRABANTIO:

A girl who was never adventurous!

Her spirit so calm and quiet that she was embarrassed by her own actions.

She fell in love with someone she would have once been afraid to even look at!

She had to be manipulated by evil tricks.

So, I insist!

He affected her with a powerful potion for this purpose,

He manipulated her.

DUKE:

But, insisting is not proof.

We need evidence.

FIRST SENATOR:

But Othello, tell us:

Did you spoil this young lady's feelings?

Or did it happen naturally?

OTHELLO:

I beg of you,

Bring the lady to this place,

And let her tell her view of me in front of her father.

If you find anything evil about me,

Then not only dismiss me from the position I hold from you,

But let your punishment be my life.

DUKE:

Bring Desdemona here.

OTHELLO:

Good man, lead them, you know the way.

Exit Iago and Attendants.

And until she arrives,
I'll honestly explain to you all
How I won this lady's heart,
And she won mine.
DUKE:
Tell us, Othello.
OTHELLO:
Her father liked me, often invited me over,
And always asked me about my life.
He wanted to know about the battles I've fought and more.
I told him everything, going back to when I was a boy,
All the way to the moment he asked me to share,
Where I spoke of terrible disasters,
Being captured by a terrible enemy,
And sold as a slave, how I gained my freedom,
And what I learned from my journeys.
Hearing all this,
Desdemona was deeply interested.
Even though matters of the home would pull her away,
As soon as she could finish her tasks,
She'd come back, and with eager ears,
Would enjoy my stories. Noting this,
I chose the right moment, and found a respectful way
To understand her love and
I then expanded on all my travels.
17 She'd heard bits and pieces before,
But never a full story from me.
I agreed to tell her,
And often her tears would flow
As I recounted some of the heartbreaks of my youth.
When my tale was told, she greeted it with a wealth of sighs.
She said it was all so wild and sad.

She thanked me and requested

That if I knew anyone who loved her,

That I should train him to tell my story and win her over.

With that, I moved forward:

She loved me because of the dangers I'd faced,

And I loved her because she felt compassion for them.

This was the only magic I used.

Here comes the woman herself.

Let her tell you.

Desdemona, Iago, and assistants enter.

DUKE:

I think this story would also have gotten my daughter's heart.

Good Brabantio, try to make the best of what happens next.

BRABANTIO:

Please let her speak.

If she admits that she was a willing participant in the relationship,

I'll take the blame,

Even if it means my downfall.

But if it's not my fault,

Then the blame falls on the man.

Come over here, my dear girl.

Do you understand who you are supposed

To be loyal to in this grand gathering?

DESDEMONA:

My respected father,

I understand and recognize my duty.

To you, I owe my life and education.

Both have taught me to respect you.

You hold authority, and until now,

I have been your daughter.

But this man is now my husband.

Even with all the devotion my mother showed you,

Choosing you above her own father,

I now pledge the same affection for my husband, the Moor.
BRABANTIO:
May God be with you!
I have said all there is to say.
If your highness will allow me,
Let's move on to public matters.
Come here, Moor.
I give you, with all my heart,
My daughter because I know you already have her affection.
I'm glad I don't have any other children because
Your union might make me overprotective.
I have done all there is to do, my lord.
DUKE:
Let's be like Brabantio in his acceptance
And give a piece of advice.
This positive message may help
The young couple gain everyone's approval.
You cannot save what destiny has taken away.
BRABANTIO:
Even if we are betrayed by the Turks in Cyprus,
We haven't truly lost as long as we can still smile.
There is no true justice for a person that carries
Both the sentence and sorrow,
Weighed down by grief with little patience to spare.
Words, whether sugar-coated or harsh,
Have a power when they sway in two different directions.
But words are just words; I have never heard...
May it please you, let's move on to matters of state.
DUKE:
The Turks are preparing a significant attack on Cyprus.
Othello, you are most familiar with the strength of the place.
Even though we have a highly capable stand-in there,
Public opinion favors you:
You must be ready for a tough mission.

OTHELLO:

Esteemed senators,

The harsh demands of war have become routine for me,

I acknowledge and I commit

To these upcoming wars against the Turks.

With respect to your power,

I request suitable arrangements for my wife.

DUKE:

If you wish,

Let her father decide this.

BRABANTIO:

I refuse.

OTHELLO:

So do I.

DESDEMONA:

And I. I wouldn't want to live there,

To cause my father discomfort

By constantly being in his sight. Kind duke,

Listen to my appeal.

DUKE:

What do you wish, Desdemona?

DESDEMONA:

That I loved the Moor to live with him,

My heart's been conquered

Fully by the character of my husband.

I saw Othello's character and

I devoted my soul and fortunes.

So, honored lords, if I am left behind,

A symbol of peace, while he goes off to war,

The reasons I love him will be taken from me,

And I would be very sad in his absence. Let me go with him.

OTHELLO:

Let her have your permission.

Swear with me, heaven, I don't wish for this

To indulge my passions,

But to support her wishes.

DUKE:

Let it be as you privately decide,

Whether she stays or goes.

The matter requires quick thinking,

And speed must answer it.

FIRST SENATOR:

You must leave tonight.

OTHELLO:

With all my heart.

DUKE:

At nine in the morning we'll meet again.

Othello, leave some officer behind,

And he will bring your orders to you,

With other necessities of quality and importance

As concerns you.

OTHELLO:

If it pleases your grace, my trusted assistant,

A man of honesty and reliability,

To his supervision I trust my wife,

Along with everything else you, your grace,

Think should be sent along after me.

DUKE:

Let it be so. Goodnight to everyone.

FIRST SENATOR:

Goodbye, brave Moor, treat Desdemona kindly.

BRABANTIO:

Take care of her, Moor. If you have the eyes to see:

She's deceived her father, and she might deceive you.

Exit Duke, Senators, Officers, and others.

OTHELLO:

I bet my life on her honesty! Trustworthy Iago,

I must leave my Desdemona with you.

Please, let your wife look after her.—
Come on, Desdemona, I have just an hour
To spend with you.

Exit Othello and Desdemona.

RODERIGO:

Iago—

IAGO:

What?

RODERIGO:

What should I do, do you think?

IAGO:

Why, go to bed and sleep.

RODERIGO:

I'll drown myself right now.

IAGO:

If you do, I'll never like you afterward. Why, you foolish man!

RODERIGO:

It's foolishness to live when living is torture.

We have permission to die when death becomes our cure.

IAGO:

Oh, that's awful!

I'd never drown myself for the love of an ordinary girl.

RODERIGO:

What can I do? I admit it's embarrassing how carried away I am,
but I just can't help myself.

IAGO:

Help yourself? Nonsense! It's up to us how we are. Our bodies are
like gardens, and our will is like the gardener. If we want to grow
nettles or lettuce, plant hyssop and pull out thyme, fill it with one
type of herb or mix it up with many, leave it barren or nurture it with
hard work, well, that's entirely up to us. If we didn't have reason to
balance out our desires, we would get into all sorts of ridiculous
behavior. But we can use reason to cool our hot tempers and our
animal desires. Love is kind of like this.

RODERIGO:

That is not true.

IAGO:

This is just physical desire and an impulse decision. Come on, act like a man. Suicide? I've declared myself your friend, and I am bound to you by your worthiness. I can't help you more than I can now. Build up your wealth. Go for the battles. Disguise yourself with a fake beard. I urge, fill up your cash. It's unlikely that Desdemona will keep loving the Moor for long. Again, stash away money for that time. And I doubt he'll continue loving her. It was a fiery start, and you'll see an equal end—again, stuff your pockets with money. These Moors are fickle in their desires. Load up your stash. What tastes as sweet as honey to him now will soon be as bitter as poison. She'll want someone younger and she'll soon see the mistake she made. So, fill up your bank account. If you insist on ruining yourself, do it in a more respectable way than drowning. Make all the money you can. If my cunning, and everything in my power, can overcome the simple promise between that Moor and the clever Venetian, you'll have her. So, make money! Forget about drowning! That's the worst path. You'd rather risk getting caught in your pursuit of happiness than drown and lose her.

RODERIGO:

Can I rely on your plans to come true?

IAGO:

You can trust me. Now, go and gather your funds. I've told you again and again, I despise the Moor. My determination is strong and yours should be too. Together, we should seek revenge against him. Let's fool him through the events that will unfold with time. So, hurry and gather your money. We can discuss this further tomorrow. Goodbye.

RODERIGO:

Where do we meet in the morning?

IAGO:

At my place.

RODERIGO:

I'll be there early.

IAGO:

Alright, goodbye. Listen, Roderigo?

RODERIGO:

What is it?

IAGO:

No more talk about drowning, okay?

RODERIGO:

I'm not the same. I'll sell all my property.

Exit.

IAGO:

This is how I always take advantage of people.

It would be a waste of my knowledge

If I used my time with such a fool

Without gaining amusement and benefit. I hate the Moor,

And rumor has it he has been after my wife.

I don't know if it's true,

But because of this suspicion,

I'll act as if it is. I am held in high esteem by him,

And this works well towards my plans.

Cassio is a worthy man. Now let's see,

How I can take his position and bolster my determination,

By being extra two-faced? Yes, let's see.

After some time, I will hint to Othello

That Cassio is too friendly with his wife.

Cassio has a charming personality,

And can easily trick women.

The Moor is honest and straightforward,

He believes men to be truthful, unless they give him reason to

suspect them.

25   He can be easily manipulated,

Like a donkey led by the nose.

I've got it.

Darkness and looming danger must reveal this terrible secret to the world.

Exit.

ACT II

SCENE 1. A SEAPORT IN CYPRUS. A PLATFORM

 [ENTER MONTANO AND TWO GENTLEMEN.]

MONTANO:
Can you see anything from the shore out at sea?
FIRST GENTLEMAN:
Not a thing. The sea is a mess.
I can't spot a single sail between the sky and the sea.
MONTANO:
It feels like the wind has let out a loud cry over land.
If it's causing such craziness,
I wonder if the strongest of oak ships can hold against its force.
What could this mean?
SECOND GENTLEMAN:
The Turkish fleet could be separated.
The angry waves appear to strike the clouds,
They splash, the waves whipped up by the wind, monstrous in size,
I've never seen such a disturbing sight on the agitated sea.

MONTANO:

If the Turkish fleet

Isn't protected and safely harbored, they'll surely capsize.

Surviving this is impossible.

Enter a Third Gentleman.

THIRD GENTLEMAN:

News, guys! Our battles are over.

The brutal storm damaged the Turks

To the point where their mission is over. A noble Venetian ship

Has sent word of severe destruction and suffering

Throughout most of their fleet.

MONTANO:

What? Is this true?

THIRD GENTLEMAN:

Indeed, the ship has docked here,

It's from Verona. Michael Cassio,

Who serves under the Moor, Othello, in war,

Has arrived, while Othello remains at sea,

He's fully in charge here in Cyprus.

MONTANO:

I'm glad to hear it. Cassio is a great leader.

THIRD GENTLEMAN:

Cassio tells us about the defeat of the Turks,

Yet he seems concerned, praying for the safety of Othello.

They had to part ways due to a terrible storm.

MONTANO:

I hope he's safe.

I have served under him and he is an excellent leader.

Let's go to the harbor and see the incoming ship.

We can continue our lookout for the brave Othello.

THIRD GENTLEMAN:

We're expecting more arrivals any minute now.

Enter Cassio.

CASSIO:

Thank you for your trust in Othello!

I pray that the heavens protect him from danger.

I lost sight of him in the dangerous sea.

MONTANO:

Is his ship well made?

CASSIO:

Yes, his ship is strong and has a skilled captain.

Therefore, my worry is not so bad and I still hold out hope.

A call from afar: "A sail, a sail, a sail!" Enter a Messenger.

CASSIO:

What's the commotion?

MESSENGER:

The townsfolk are on the beach shouting "A sail!"

CASSIO:

I hope it's Othello.

A gunshot.

SECOND GENTLEMAN:

It's a celebratory shot! Must be our friends.

CASSIO:

Could you go and find out who has arrived?

SECOND GENTLEMAN:

I will.

Exits.

MONTANO:

So, Lieutenant Cassio, is your general married?

28

CASSIO:

Luckily, he's won over a woman

Who is beyond description and fame.

She is beautiful.

Enter Second Gentleman.

What's the news? Who has arrived?

SECOND GENTLEMAN:

It's Iago, assistant to the general.

CASSIO:

He's had a smooth and lucky journey.

Even storms, dangerous seas, and forceful winds,

The jagged rocks, and gathering sands,

That often threaten to hinder innocent ships,

Seem to appreciate beauty, letting pass

The wonderful Desdemona.

MONTANO:

Who is she?

CASSIO:

The woman I mentioned who is wife to our great captain.

She was left in the care of the bold Iago,

Who has arrived here ahead of our expectations.

Mighty God, protect Othello,

And fill his sails with your powerful winds,

So he may bring joy to this place with his impressive arrival.

Ignite his passion in Desdemona's arms,

Renew our spirits,

And bring comfort to all of Cyprus!

Enter Desdemona, Iago, Roderigo, and Emilia.

See, behold,

The treasure of the ship has come.

Citizens of Cyprus, show her your respect.

Greetings to you, lady! May the grace of heaven,

Surround you from all sides!

DESDEMONA:

I am grateful, brave Cassio.

What news can you share about my husband?

CASSIO:

He has not yet arrived, but I know

That he's well and will be arriving shortly.

DESDEMONA:

Oh, but I worry! How did we get separated?

[Within.] A ship, a ship!

CASSIO:

The dangerous sea and skies
Split our group. But, listen! A ship.

Guns within.

SECOND GENTLEMAN:
This ship is friendly.
CASSIO:
Look out for news.

Exit Gentleman.

Welcome, wise soldier. *[To Emilia.]* Welcome, madam.
Iago, it's just my nature to be courteous.

Kissing her.

IAGO:
Sir, if she gave you as much of her kisses
As she gives me of her words,
You would have enough.
DESDEMONA:
Oh, she doesn't talk too much.
IAGO:
In truth, she talks a great deal.
I notice this most when I want to rest.
EMILIA:
You don't have much reason to say that.
IAGO:
Come now, come now!. You women are like outdoor paintings,
Bells in your living rooms, wild-cats in your kitchens,
Saints when you're wronged, devils when offended,
Actresses in your chores, and housewives in bed.
DESDEMONA:
Stop it!
IAGO:
No, it's true!
You rise to have fun, and go to bed to work.
EMILIA:
Just stop talking.

IAGO:

No, I won't.

DESDEMONA:

What would you say about me if you had something nice to say?

IAGO:

Oh kind lady, don't ask me to,

I'm much too critical.

DESDEMONA:

Come on, test me. Did someone go to the harbor?

IAGO:

Yes, ma'am.

DESDEMONA:

I'm not happy. How would you compliment me?

IAGO:

I'm thinking about it it, but really,

My creativity comes from my head like a thread.

It pulls out everything. Here's what it might say:

If a woman is beautiful and smart,

Her beauty is used by everyone,

But she herself uses her intelligence.

DESDEMONA:

Well said! What if she's witty but not beautiful?

IAGO:

If she's not beautiful, but witty,

She'll find someone who complements her.

DESDEMONA:

This keeps getting worse.

EMILIA:

What if she's pretty but not very smart?

IAGO:

A beautiful woman is never foolish,

Because even her foolishness could help her.

DESDEMONA:

What kind of compliment do you have

For a woman who's neither smart nor beautiful?
IAGO:
Even a woman who's not bright or pretty engages
In actions that smart and beautiful people do.
DESDEMONA:
That's absurd!
But what compliment could you give a truly deserving woman?
A woman who could face even the harshest criticism.
IAGO:
She who was always beautiful and never arrogant,
Who could talk when she wanted to,
Who had enough wealth but was never flashy,
Who restrained her desires yet said, "Now I may"
When she was free to do as she pleased.
A woman who could...
Know to be patient and let her anger go.
She who could think yet never spill her thoughts,
See admirers trailing yet never turn back,
She was a unique being, if ever such existed—
DESDEMONA:
What?
IAGO:
She could nourish fools and talk about silly things.
DESDEMONA:
What a lame conclusion!
Don't follow his lessons.
Emilia, even if he's your husband.
—What's your opinion, Cassio?
Isn't he a disrespectful advisor?
CASSIO:
He's direct, ma'am.
You might find him more appealing as a soldier than as a scholar.
IAGO:
[Aside.] He holds her hand. Right on, whisper.

With as little a trap as this, I'll catch a big fish like Cassio.

Yes, smile at her, that's it.

I will catch you using your own flirtation.

Tricks like these might just cause you to lose your position,

Trumpets within.

That's Othello's trumpet, I know it.

CASSIO:

You're right.

DESDEMONA:

Let's go welcome him.

CASSIO:

Look, here he comes!

Othello and his entourage enter.

OTHELLO:

Oh, my beautiful!

DESDEMONA:

My dear Othello!

OTHELLO:

It fills me with great wonder to see my happiness.

To see you standing before me, you are the joy of my life!

If after every storm there comes such peace,

May the winds blow until they've stirred the slumber of death!

This is the perfect moment, because I'm afraid

My happiness is so complete

That no other joy can compare to this one

And I don't know what the future holds.

DESDEMONA:

May heaven keep

Our love and happiness!

OTHELLO:

Amen to that, my love!

I can't express my happiness enough.

It overwhelms me; it's too much joy:

And this, and this, will be the biggest disagreements

They kiss.

That our hearts will ever have!

IAGO:

[Aside.] Oh, you are in harmony now,

But I'll alter the notes that produce this music,

As true as I am.

OTHELLO:

Let's go to the castle.—

All, our battles are over, the Turks have been defeated.

How is my old friend of this island?

Darling, you'll be well received in Cyprus;

I have discovered a lot of love here.

—I beg you, good Iago,

Go to the bay and unload my things.

Bring the captain to the castle.

He is a good man, and his honor

Demands great respect.—Let's go, Desdemona,

We meet again in Cyprus.

Exit Othello, Desdemona, and Attendants.

IAGO:

Meet me quickly at the dock.

Come here. If you're brave--as they say,

Even low men find courage when they're in love-

Hear me out.

The lieutenant has guard duty tonight.

First, I must tell you this: Desdemona is head over heels for him.

RODERIGO:

For him? No way.

IAGO:

Listen carefully, let your soul absorb this. Consider how she first loved the Moor, all because of his grand tales and outrageous lies. Do you think she'll continue to love him for his empty chatter? Don't let your wise heart believe it. She needs visual fulfillment. What pleasure will she find in looking at the devil? When the passion is dulled by the acts of love, there has to be more—kindness, age compatibility, manners, looks—all things the Moor lacks. Now, without these necessities, her delicate feelings will feel offended, she'll start to dislike the Moor, her own nature will make her realize this and push her towards a second choice. Now sir, given this truth (which is indeed a convincing and straightforward explanation), who is so much in line for this good fortune as Cassio is? A deceitful man, and extremely persuasive, he's as honest as he needs to be to appear civil and gentle. However, I know what he's waiting for. Who else could it be? No one, absolutely no one! A clever and cunning trickster, an opportunist. He can pretend to see an advantage or potential benefit, even when there isn't one: he's an evil trickster! Plus, he's good-looking, young, and checks all the boxes that the naive and inexperienced look for. A totally despicable trickster and it seems the woman has already noticed him.

RODERIGO:

She's blessed, you say? Nonsense! Her nectar is mere grape juice. If she truly had a blessed nature, she would not have fallen for the Moor. All this talk of blessedness is silly. Didn't you notice how she was caressing his hand? Didn't you mark that?

RODERIGO:

Yes, I saw that. But that's just a friendly gesture.

IAGO:

No, it's more than that. It's a foreshadowing, a sign of the incoming storm of passion and unclean thoughts. Their meeting was so intimate, you could see their breaths mingle together. It's clearly a hint to something more, Roderigo! When such signs are so obviously presented, what follows can only be the dreadful main event, the culmination of all these sins. Bah! Listen, just follow my lead. I brought you here from Venice. Keep an eye on the situation tonight. I'll guide you. Cassio doesn't know you. I'll stay close. Find some way to provoke him. Speak too loudly, question his orders, or choose any other technique that suits the moment as it unfolds.

RODERIGO:

Alright.

IAGO:

Sure, he's hot-tempered and might react violently, possibly hitting you with his weapon. And that's what we want: provoke him into this. From there I can stir unrest among the soldiers of Cyprus who will, after this event, will only be interested in working for a leader like you. Thus, with this move, you'll be a step closer to your dreams. So, just follow my advice, and remove this issue efficiently, without which there is no path to success.

RODERIGO:

I'll do this if I can find the opportunity.

IAGO:

That's the spirit. Meet me later at the fortress: there are tasks I need to take care of. Goodbye for now.

RODERIGO:

Goodbye.

Exit.

IAGO:

Cassio's love for her seems genuine.
And she, too, is likely interested in him.
The Moor, although I can't stand him,
Is undeniably loyal and truly caring,
And I can picture him being a sweet husband to Desdemona.
I must confess, I have feelings for her too.
Not solely out of attraction,
But also to fuel my vengeance.
I have a sneaking suspicion the Moor
has intruded into my life somehow and taken my place.
This thought eats away at me like a poison.
Nothing will soothe my soul
Until I am on equal terms with him, an eye for an eye.
Or, if I can't accomplish that, I at least want to make him
Wildly jealous.

That's my game plan and this unsuspecting pawn from Venice
will help me play it.

37   I'll use Michael Cassio's habit
Of jumping into action against him,
Setting him up in such a scenario
Since I do not trust him either.
I'll manipulate the situation
In such a way that Othello
Will believe that I've saved him
From being made a fool,
While I disturb his calm and peace
Up to the point of insanity.
It's planned.

Exit.

SCENE 11. A STREET

 [Enter Othello's Herald (Messenger) with an announcement.]

HERALD:

Our brave and honorable leader, Othello, has some instructions based on new information that's just arrived. The Turkish fleet has been completely destroyed! He wants everyone to celebrate this victory: some by dancing, some by lighting bonfires. Anyone can choose whatever activity makes them happy. But that's not all! It's also time for Othello's wedding celebration! Everyone is free to eat and party from five in the evening until eleven at night. May God bless the island of Cyprus and our noble leader, Othello!

Exit.

SCENE III. A HALL IN THE CASTLE

 [Enter Othello, Desdemona, Cassio and their followers.]

OTHELLO:
Michael, make sure you oversee tonight's guard.
We need to stay in control.
CASSIO:
Iago knows what must be done.
Despite that, I will ensure that it all goes well.
OTHELLO:
Iago is a very trustworthy man.
Michael, have a good night.
And first thing tomorrow morning,
I'd like to have a chat with you. *[To Desdemona.]*
My dear love,
We've embarked upon a journey,
The benefits of which are yet to come;
Many gains still lie ahead for you and me.
Have a good night.

Exit Othello, Desdemona, and their followers. Iago enters.

CASSIO:

Welcome, Iago. We need to start the security watch.

IAGO:

It's not time yet. It isn't ten o'clock yet. Othello made us start early because he loves his Desdemona and wants to spend time with her. We shouldn't blame him though, as they have not spent much time together yet.

CASSIO:

She is indeed an elegant lady.

IAGO:

And you can be sure, full of zest.

CASSIO:

She certainly is refreshingly charming and gentle.

IAGO:

What expressive eyes she has! It seems they invite interaction.

CASSIO:

Her eyes are captivating, but also quite modest.

IAGO:

And when she speaks, isn't it like a call for affection? Like she's asking you?

CASSIO:

She is undoubtedly perfect.

IAGO:

Well, best wishes to their relationship! Michael, I have some wine here, and some local buddies outside who would love to toast to Othello's health.

CASSIO:

Not tonight, Iago. I really don't want to drink too much. I really wish that there were some other way we could enjoy ourselves.

IAGO:

Oh, they're our friends! Just one drink! I'll drink on your behalf.

CASSIO:

I've had only one drink tonight, and even that one was watered down, but look at the effect it's having. I can't handle alcohol well, and I wouldn't dare to push my limit any further.

IAGO:

Come on, man! This is a night of celebration. The guys want this.

CASSIO:

Where are they?

IAGO:

Right here at the door. Please, invite them in.

CASSIO:

I'll do it, but I'm not really comfortable with this.

Exit.

IAGO:

If I can get him to take just one more drink,

Added to what he's had already tonight,

He'll become as irritable and argumentative.

Now, lovesick Roderigo,

Who is so obsessed he's not thinking straight,

Has drunk himself into fantasy about Desdemona tonight,

And he's on guard duty. Three young gentlemen of Cyprus,

Honorable and proud,

Who take their roles very seriously,

True representatives of this warrior island,

I've shaped them with alcohol tonight.

They, too, are on duty. Now, among this bunch of drunks,

I need to get Cassio to do something

That may offend the people here. But here they come:

If things turn out the way I have imagined,

My ship sails smoothly, benefitting from both the current and the breeze.

Enter Cassio, Montano, and Gentlemen; followed by a Servant carrying wine.

CASSIO:

Honestly, they have already raised my spirits.

MONTANO:

Indeed, just a bit, not more than half a bottle, like a true soldier.

IAGO:

Bring more wine!

Sings.

And let the small cup go clink, clink,
    And let me the small cup go clink, clink!
    A soldier is brave,
    Oh, life is but a brief wave,
    So, why not let a soldier savor his drink.

Bring some wine, boys!

CASSIO:

By all that's holy, that's an excellent song.

IAGO:

I picked it up in England, where indeed they are really good at drinking. Your Danish, your German, and your beer-bellied Dutchman—drink up!—are nothing compared to an Englishman.

CASSIO:

Is an Englishman truly that adept at handling his drink?

IAGO:

Well, he can drink your Danish man under the table with ease. He doesn't break a sweat to defeat your German. He can make your Dutcman throw up before the next bottle can even be filled.

CASSIO:

To our leader's health!

MONTANO:

I'm in favor of that, lieutenant, and I'll raise a glass to that.

IAGO:

Oh beautiful England!

Sings.

King Stephen was a nobleman,
    His pants cost him only a dollar!

He thought they were a touch too expensive,
With that he yelled at the tailor.
He was a man of high standing,
And you are of lower class.
It is pride that brings the nation down!
Put your cloak on your shoulders 'round!

Bring some wine!

CASSIO:

Honestly, this song is even better than the other.

IAGO:

Would you like to hear it again?

CASSIO:

My interpretation is that anyone who acts in such a way is unworthy of his position. After all, God is above everyone and decides who will be saved and who will not.

IAGO:

That's indeed correct, honored lieutenant.

CASSIO:

Speaking for myself, and not meaning to offend the general or any men of high ranking, I aim to be among those who are saved.

IAGO:

And I have the same aspiration, lieutenant.

CASSIO:

But, if you'll excuse me, I should be saved first, for the rank of a lieutenant comes before that of an officer. Let's put an end to this topic. Let's deal with more important matters. May we be forgiven for our sins! Gentlemen, let's focus on our duties. Don't mistakenly perceive me as intoxicated. This is my assistant, my right hand, and this is my left. I promise you, I'm not drunk. I can stand and speak fine.

ALL:

Extremely well-said!

CASSIO:

Well then, maybe I don't sound too drunk.

He leaves.

MONTANO:

To the lookout point, sirs. Let's establish our watch now.

IAGO:

Look at the man who just left.

He's a soldier capable enough

To serve alongside Cæsar and provide guidance.

His only fault is perfectly balanced with his virtue.

It's a shame, really.

I worry that the trust Othello puts in him,

At a weak moment, might unsettle our island.

MONTANO:

Does he behave like this often?

IAGO:

This seems to be a routine occurrence before he sleeps. He could potentially stay awake twice the usual amount if alcohol doesn't send him to sleep.

MONTANO:

It might be best if the general was made aware of it.

Maybe he doesn't see it, or his good-hearted nature...

Values more the good traits exhibited by Cassio,

And seems to ignore his vices. Isn't that so?

Enter Roderigo.

IAGO

[Aside to Roderigo]: Hey there, Roderigo.

Follow after lieutenant Cassio, will you?

Exit Roderigo.

MONTANO:

It's a dreadful thought that the honorable Othello

Should risk such an important role as his second-in-command

To someone with such a weaknesses for alcohol.

It would be the right thing to bring this up

With Othello.

IAGO:

I wouldn't do it, not for anything on this beautiful island.

I genuinely like Cassio and would prefer to help him.

But, listen! Do you hear something?

There's a cry from off stage: "Help! Help!" Cassio enters, driving Roderigo
in front of him.

CASSIO:

How dare you, you crook, you mischief-maker!

MONTANO:

What's happening, lieutenant?

CASSIO:

A lowly man tries to teach me my job!? Yeah, right!

RODERIGO:

Me?

CASSIO:

Are you mouthing off, scoundrel?

Cassio hits Roderigo.

MONTANO:

Hold on, good lieutenant,

I beg you, sir, hold back.

CASSIO:

Let me go, sir,

Or I'll knock you senseless.

MONTANO:

Calm down, you're drunk.

CASSIO:

Drunk?

They begin to fight.

IAGO:

[Aside to Roderigo.]

Get out of here! Raise the cry of a rebellion.

Exit Roderigo.

For the love of God, gentlemen.

Help! Lieutenant, sir, Montano, sir,

Help, everyone! This is a terrible watch!

A bell rings.

What's that bell ringing? — Alarm, what on earth!
The town is waking up. For God's sake, lieutenant, stop,
Or you'll disgrace yourself forever.

Othello enters with attendants.

OTHELLO:

What's going on here?

MONTANO:

Curses, I'm still bleeding, I'm hurt badly.

OTHELLO:

Stop, for your lives!

IAGO:

Stop, everyone!

Have you forgotten sense and duty?

Stop! The general is speaking to you! Stop, stop!

OTHELLO:

What's going on? Where is this coming from?

For the love of decency, stop this savage fight.

Whoever moves next to fight for his own anger

Shows no value for his life and disrupts the peace.

What's going on, everyone?

Trustworthy Iago, who looks terrified,

Speak, who started this? Tell me.

IAGO:

I don't know. We were all friends just moments ago

I can't pinpoint

What sparked this fight.

I wish I hadn't been part of it!

OTHELLO:

What happened, Michael, to make you act this way?

CASSIO:

Please, forgive me. I can't talk about it.

OTHELLO:

Honorable Montano, you're usually calm.
What's happened
That you would risk tarnishing your reputation like this,
And give up the respect you have earned?
Why were you brawling at night? Answer me.

MONTANO:

Honorable Othello, I am seriously injured.
I did not say or do anything wrong tonight,
Unless sometimes taking care of oneself is a bad thing,
And defending ourselves is wrong
When someone attacks us.

OTHELLO:

My passion, having clouded my better judgement,
Tries to lead the way.
Tell me how this dreadful fight started.
Who initiated it?
This one will lose my favour.
Who would have personal and home quarrels,
At night, and near the court and secure venues?
It's monstrous. Iago, who started it?

MONTANO:

If you provide more or less than the truth,
You're not a true soldier.

IAGO:

Be careful how you address me.
I'd rather have this tongue cut from my mouth
Than cause any harm to Michael Cassio.
Yet I've convinced myself, to tell the truth
Won't harm him. So here it is, general:
Montano and I were in the middle of a conversation,
When a man ran by crying out for help,
And Cassio was chasing him with a drawn sword,
Ready to strike him down. Sir, this gentleman
Steps in to calm down Cassio.

I followed the man who was crying for help,

Worried that his loud screams

Would frighten the people of the town. He was fast,

And outran me. I came back because

I heard the sound of falling swords.

When I returned, I found them fighting close range.

I can't report more about this issue.

But men are men. The best sometimes forget themselves.

OTHELLO:

Iago, I know

Your honesty and friendship are trying to downplay this issue,

To protect Cassio. Cassio, I care about you,

But you will no longer be my officer.

Enter Desdemona, accompanied by others.

I will use you as a warning.

DESDEMONA:

What's happening?

OTHELLO:

Everything is okay now, darling.

Montano is led away.

Iago, calm down those troubled by this terrible fight.

Come, Desdemona.

Everyone exits except Iago and Cassio.

IAGO:

What, Lieutenant, are you hurt?

CASSIO:

Yes, beyond any doctor's help.

CASSIO:

No, don't even say that!

CASSIO:

My reputation, my reputation, my reputation! Oh, I've lost my reputation! I've lost the most important part of myself, and what's left is disgraceful. My good name, Iago, my good name!

IAGO:

Honestly, I thought you were physically hurt. That would be easier to mend than reputation. Reputation is often an empty and false idea, often gained without earning it and lost without deserving it. You haven't lost your reputation, unless you believe you've lost it yourself. Don't worry, there's a way to get back in good graces with the general. You are just temporarily out of favor, a punishment more strategic than hateful, akin to hitting a harmless dog to scare off a threatening lion. Just apologize to him again and he'll forgive you.

CASSIO:

I'd rather be rejected than to betray such a good leader with my irresponsible, drunken, and thoughtless behavior. Was it me who was talking nonsense? Arguing? Being aggressive? Cursing? And holding pointless conversations with my own reflection? Oh, you unseen force of wine, if you have no name, let's just call you devil!

IAGO:

Who was it that you chased after with your sword? What did he do to you?

CASSIO:

I don't know.

IAGO:

Is that possible?

CASSIO:

I remember bits and pieces, but nothing clearly. A fight, but not the reason. Oh God, why do men let alcohol, an enemy, into their system to rob them of their senses! That we should turn ourselves into monsters while seeking joy, pleasure, and approval!

IAGO:

IAGO:

Alright, you seem to have recovered nicely. How'd you bounce back?

CASSIO:

It's like the monster of drunkenness stepped aside for the

monster of anger. One flaw uncovers another, making me despise my own character.

IAGO:

Easy, you're being too hard on yourself. Considering the situation, the location, and the nature of our surroundings, I genuinely wish this never happened, but it's already done, so you need to fix it for your own sake.

CASSIO:

I'll ask for my rank back, but I know he thinks I'm a drunk! Even if I had as many mouths as the mythical Hydra, such a response would silence them all. To go from being a sensible man, to a fool, then to a beast. How bizarre! Every excessive drink is cursed, and within it lives a demon.

IAGO:

Relax, good wine is basically a close friend, as long as you use it wisely. Don't curse it anymore. And, my noble lieutenant, I feel you believe I care for you.

CASSIO:

Your actions have proven as much, sir. --Me, drunk?

IAGO:

Any man can get drunk at times, including you. Here's what you should do. The general's wife is in charge. I say this because he's completely captivated by her grace and beauty. Be honest with her. Ask for her help to get you back in your good position. She is so kind, so willing, so generous, that she views it as a failure on her part if she doesn't do more than she's asked. The fractured relationship between you and her husband, ask her to mend. Bet my luck against anything, your relationship will become stronger than before.

CASSIO:

That's good advice.

IAGO:

I assure you, it's given with the sincerest of intentions.

CASSIO:

I appreciate that. First thing in the morning, I'll appeal to the virtuous Desdemona to speak for me. I've hit rock bottom if they reject me.

IAGO:

You're on the right track. Goodnight, lieutenant, I need to go on watch.

CASSIO:

Goodnight, trustworthy Iago.

Exit.

IAGO:

And who would dare to say that I'm being deceitful here?

This advice that I'm giving is free and sincere,

Pragmatic in thought, and it's the strategy

To win the Moor's favor again? Because it's fairly easy

For the cooperative Desdemona to succeed

In any honest request. She's as abundant

As the free elements. And then, for her

To win over the Moor, even if he had to give up his faith,

His soul is so captivated by her love

50   SHE CAN SHAPE, unshape, do whatever she wants.

How am I a villain to urge Cassio along this same path,

Which leads directly to his benefit?

While this naive guy pleads with Desdemona to rebuild his fortune,

And she pleads for him to the Moor,

I'll infect Othello's ear with this toxic idea:

I'll make Othello think she's doing that just so she can have Cassio around.

And the more she tries to help Cassio,

The more she'll damage her relationship with the Moor.

I'll twist her good nature into something foul.

I'll weave the trap that'll entangle them all.

Enter Roderigo.

What's up, Roderigo?

RODERIGO:

I'm just trailing along here

I'm almost out of money,

I've been really beaten up tonight.

Maybe I'll head back to Venice.

IAGO:

How unfortunate are those who don't have patience!

What wound ever healed quickly?

Cassio may have beat you,

Yet, you have gotten Cassio fired!

Hold your horses for a bit.

Head to bed.

You'll find out more later.

Roderigo leaves.

There's two things that need to be done.

My wife has to persuade Cassio to speak to her boss.

I'll encourage her to do so.

In the meantime, I'll distract the Moor,

And lead him over right when he spots Cassio

Chatting up his wife. Yes, that's the plan.

Don't let the plan go dull by being too cold or slow.

Exit.

ACT III

SCENE 1. CYPRUS. BEFORE THE CASTLE

 [Enter Cassio and musicians.]

CASSIO:

Musicians, perform here, I will make your effort worthwhile, something short and give a "Good morning" to the general.

Music plays. Enter a Clown.

CLOWN:

Why do your instruments sound so nasal, like they're from Naples?

FIRST MUSICIAN:

What do you mean?

CLOWN:

Are these wind instruments?

FIRST MUSICIAN:

Yes, indeed, they are.

CLOWN:

Oh, there's more to this story.

FIRST MUSICIAN:

What's the story?

CLOWN:

By every wind instrument I've ever seen, that's the story. But listen: Here's some money for you. The general enjoys your music but desires you to stop playing right now, as a favor.

FIRST MUSICIAN:

Of course, we will stop.

CLOWN:

If you have any music that can't be heard, play that instead. But the general isn't too keen on hearing music.

FIRST MUSICIAN:

We have no such music.

CLOWN:

Then pack up quickly. Disappear, go away!

The musicians leave

CASSIO:

Did you hear that, my honest friend?

CLOWN:

No, I didn't hear your honest friend. I heard you.

CASSIO:

Please, keep your spirits high. Here's a small piece of gold for you: if the attendant to the general's wife is awake, please tell her Cassio requests a small favor of time to talk. Will you do this?

CLOWN:

She's awake, sir. If she will come here, I'll make sure to let her know.

CASSIO:

Good, my friend.

Exit Clown. Enter Iago.

Just in time, Iago.

IAGO:

Haven't you slept, then?

CASSIO:

No, why would I? It was already morning

Before we parted ways. I hope it's okay, Iago,

That I asked for your wife's help. My request to her

Is that she'd introduce me to virtuous Desdemona.

IAGO:

I'll send her to you soon,

And I'll figure out a way to distract the Moor

So you two can have a more private conversation.

CASSIO:

I appreciate that, truly.

Exit Iago.

I've never met

A person from Florence as nice and honest as him.

Enter Emilia.

EMILIA:

Good morning, Lieutenant. I'm sorry for your trouble.

The general and his wife are discussing it. She supports you.

The Moor responded that the man you harmed is quite well-known in Cyprus.

So wisely, he couldn't do anything but reject your apology.

He says he values you and doesn't need anyone else to convince him

That at some point this needs to be resolved.

CASSIO:

Even so, I'd like to ask you:

Could you give me a chance to have a short conversation

Alone with Desdemona?

EMILIA:

Of course, please, come in.

I'll arrange so you have enough time

To talk with her alone.

CASSIO:

I am grateful.

Exit.

SCENE 11. CYPRUS. A ROOM IN THE CASTLE

54 *[Enter Othello, Iago, and some gentlemen.]*

OTHELLO:
Iago, please give these letters to the ship's captain,
And through him,
Pass along my responsibilities to the city's leaders.
After you've done that, come and find me. I'll be nearby.
IAGO:
Of course, my lord, I'll do as you ask.
OTHELLO:
Now, gentlemen, shall we inspect this fortress?
GENTLEMEN:
We are at your service, sir.

Exit.

SCENE III. CYPRUS. THE GARDEN OF THE CASTLE

 [Desdemona, Cassio, and Emilia enter.]

DESDEMONA:

Cassio, I'll do right by you, using all my capabilities.

EMILIA:

Madam, please do. It pains my husband.

DESDEMONA:

That's a good man. Don't worry, Cassio,

We'll make sure you and my lord are friends again.

CASSIO:

Gracious madam,

No matter what happens to me, Michael Cassio,

Know I'm always your loyal servant.

DESDEMONA:

I know and I'm grateful. You love my husband.

You've known him for a long time.

He won't treat you unfairly.

CASSIO:

But, madam,

If this situation continues for too long,

Or doesn't improve,

He might forget our long friendship.

DESDEMONA:

Don't worry about that. In front of Emilia here,

I tell you I'll keep my promise.

I'll keep after my husband until he helps you.

So cheer up, Cassio,

I'd rather die than not help you.

Othello and Iago walk in.

EMILIA:

Madam, your husband is coming.

CASSIO:

Madam, I'm going.

DESDEMONA:

Wait, and let me speak.

CASSIO:

Madam, not right now. I am uncomfortable.

DESDEMONA:

Alright, do as you think best.

Cassio exits.

IAGO:

Hmm, I don't like that.

OTHELLO:

What did you say?

IAGO:

Nothing, my lord...I'm not sure what.

OTHELLO:

Wasn't that Cassio leaving my wife?

IAGO:

Cassio, my lord? No, I don't think he would sneak off like that,

Seeing you approach.

OTHELLO:

I believe it was him.

DESDEMONA:

What's wrong, my lord?

I've been talking to someone who's seeking your favor,

A man who suffers from your disapproval.

OTHELLO:

Who are you talking about?

DESDEMONA:

Your deputy, Cassio. Dear lord,

If I have any influence over you,

Please forgive him.

OTHELLO:

Has he just left?

DESDEMONA:

Yes, he was so upset

That part of his pain stays with me.

Please, my love, call him back.

OTHELLO:

Not now, dear Desdemona, some other time.

DESDEMONA:

But will it be soon?

OTHELLO:

The sooner, my dear, for you.

DESDEMONA:

Will it be tonight at dinner?

OTHELLO:

No, not tonight.

DESDEMONA:

Tomorrow for lunch then?

OTHELLO:

I will not be home for lunch.

DESDEMONA:

Then tomorrow night, or Tuesday morning,

Tuesday noon, or night, Wednesday morning?

DESDEMONA:

Don't let it

Be more than three days. I trust he is sorry.

And yet his mistake hardly deserves such a huge punishment.

When will he return?

OTHELLO:

Enough. Let him come whenever he wishes.

I'm not keeping anything from you.

DESDEMONA:

This should be easy.

This is not a request

That challenges your love towards me

And is therefore difficult to grant.

OTHELLO:

I won't deny you anything.

But I beg you to grant me this one thing,

To leave me alone for a little while on this matter.

DESDEMONA:

Goodbye, my lord.

OTHELLO:

Goodbye, my Desdemona. I'll come to you soon.

DESDEMONA:

Emilia, come. Do as you please.

Whatever you think, I will obey.

Desdemona exits with Emilia.

OTHELLO:

Wonderful woman!

I do love her!

When I stop loving her,

It would mean chaos has returned.

IAGO:

My commendable lord,—

58 **OTHELLO:**

What are you suggesting, Iago?

IAGO:

Did Michael Cassio know about your love

For Desdemona when you were courting her?

OTHELLO:

Yes, he did, from the very beginning. Why are you asking?

IAGO:

Just curious. Nothing more, really.

OTHELLO:

Curious about what, Iago?

IAGO:

I just didn't think he knew her that well.

OTHELLO:

Oh yes, he was often around when we were together.

IAGO:

Really?

OTHELLO:

Really? Of course, really.

Do you sense something wrong with that?

Do you think he's not a good man?

IAGO:

Good man, my lord?

OTHELLO:

Good man? Yes, indeed, a good man.

IAGO:

My lord, as far as I know.

OTHELLO:

What's your opinion?

IAGO:

My opinion, my lord?

OTHELLO:

Why are you repeating my questions?

It's like there's something you're afraid to say.

You furrow your brow as if you are concealing
Some terrible idea.
If you truly care about me, tell me what you're thinking.
What is your suspicion about Cassio?
IAGO:
My lord, you know I respect and care about you.
OTHELLO:
I believe you do.
But it's precisely because you're so full of love and honesty,
And you choose your words carefully that your looks scare me.
These behaviors might be a regular thing for a deceptive and disloyal person,
But for a man of integrity, like yourself, they can hint at real concerns.
Certainly, emotion should not control us.
IAGO:
Regarding Michael Cassio,
I can confidently say,
I believe he is honest.
OTHELLO:
I believe the same.
IAGO:
People should be as they appear to be.
Those who aren't, would be better off not pretending at all!
OTHELLO:
Absolutely.
IAGO:
In that case, I believe Cassio is an honest man.
OTHELLO:
But, I feel there's more to this.
Please, share your thoughts with me as they come to you.
Don't hesitate to express your deepest concerns,
No matter how bleak they are.
IAGO:

Please forgive me, my lord.

Although I am committed to fulfilling every duty,

I wish I didn't have to say such things.

OTHELLO:

Iago, you're plotting against your friend.

If you believe he's done something wrong,

but keep your thoughts hidden from him.

IAGO:

I beg you, I have a tendency towards suspicion.

It won't serve your peace of mind, your well-being,

Nor my integrity or wisdom, to let you in on my thoughts.

OTHELLO:

What are you trying to say, Iago?

IAGO:

A person's reputation, my lord,

Is the most precious thing they possess.

Those who tarnish my reputation take from me

What doesn't enrich them and leaves me truly poor.

OTHELLO:

I swear, I will know what you're thinking.

IAGO:

Even if my heart was in your hands, you couldn't...

OTHELLO:

What?

IAGO:

Just be careful, my lord, of jealousy.

Jealousy is a green-eyed beast

That mocks the love it feeds on.

The man fooled by his wife, yet sure of her love, has peace.

But sadness comes to the man who loves passionately,

While doubts and suspicion haunt him!

OTHELLO:

What misery!

IAGO:

May all the powers protect us from jealousy!

OTHELLO:

Do you think I could live a life of constant jealousy and suspicion?

No. I would cast doubts once never do it again.

Where there's goodness, these qualities are virtuous.

I will not undermine my wife's qualities due to my own insecurities.

61 Small doubts or worry of her turning against me,

Because she chose me. No, Iago,

I'll witness before I doubt. When I doubt,

Only then will I know something is wrong.

Away at once with love or jealousy!

IAGO:

I'm pleased, because now I have a reason

To show the love and respect I have for you

In a more sincere way.

To be taken advantage of because of its kindness. Watch out for it.

I know how people in our country behave.

Their strongest moral principle

Cannot avoid doing wrong,

But instead will choose to keep it a secret.

OTHELLO:

You're saying this?

IAGO:

She deceived her father when she married you.

OTHELLO:

Yes, she did.

IAGO:

Well, take this into consideration then.

She was able to put on an act so well that

Her father didn't doubt her innocence.

He thought it was witchcraft.

I humbly beg for your forgiveness
For saying such things.
I just care for you very much.
OTHELLO:
I owe you forever.
IAGO:
I see I have upset you.
OTHELLO:
Not in the least, not at all.
IAGO:
Trust me, I'm worried it has.
I hope you'll understand what's said
Comes from my love. But I can see you're affected.
It's my request that you don't interpret my words too harshly.
To bigger problems
Than just suspicion.
OTHELLO:
I will not entertain it.
IAGO:
If you do, my lord,
My words would lead to terrible things
Which I never intended. Cassio is my worthy friend.
My lord, I see that you're upset.
OTHELLO:
No, not that upset.
I don't doubt Desdemona's honesty.
IAGO:
May she live long with that honesty! And you too for thinking so!
OTHELLO:
And yet, when we consider how nature can get away from its
course—
IAGO:
Yes, that's the point. To be honest with you,
She denied so many proposals

From her own place, her own kind and social rank...
But forgive me. I fear
Her betraying her better judgement,
She may eventually compare you with her familiar standards,
And possibly regret her choice.

OTHELLO:

Goodbye, farewell:
If you see more, let me know more;
Spy on your wife. Leave me now, Iago.

IAGO: *[Getting ready to leave.]*

My lord, goodbye.

OTHELLO:

Why did I get married?
This honest man surely
Sees and knows more,
Much more, than he's telling me.

IAGO:

[Coming back.] My lord, I only wish I could help you
To investigate this matter no further.
Leave it be for the time being.
Though it makes sense for Cassio to have his position,
Because surely he does the job well...
Back off from him for a bit,
So you can have the chance to better understand him
And his true character.
Pay attention to how she acts around him
And see if she continues to plead for him.
Keep her free, I plead with you.

OTHELLO:

Don't fear my ruling.

IAGO:

I'll go now.

Exit.

OTHELLO:

This man is honest,
And knows all about people, with a wise spirit.
If I do find her unfaithful,
Even though I deeply care for her,
I'd let her go.
Maybe, because of my identity or
Because perhaps I am getting older—
I have been lied to.
If that's true, the only way
I can find peace is to hate her.
Oh, the curse of marriage.
I'd rather be a toad,
And live with the bare minimum in a dungeon,
Than share the woman I love
With others. Yet, it's the curse of the powerful,
No one is exempt from this.
Here comes Desdemona.
If she's unfaithful, then heaven plays tricks on itself!
I refuse to believe it.

Enter Desdemona and Emilia.

DESDEMONA:
Hello, my dear Othello.
Your dinner and those
Whom you invited, are waiting for you.

OTHELLO:
It's my fault.

DESDEMONA:
Why are you speaking so softly?
Aren't you feeling okay?

OTHELLO:
I have a headache.

DESDEMONA:
That's from staying up too late.
It will go away if you rest.

OTHELLO:

Your handkerchief is too small.

He tries to use it to bandage his forehead,
but it falls to the ground.

Nevermind. Let's go inside together.

DESDEMONA:

I'm very sorry that you're feeling unwell.

They exit.

EMILIA:

I'm glad I found this handkerchief.
This was her first gift from Othello.
My husband asked me to steal it many times.
And now I'm going to borrow it and
give it to Iago. I don't know what he'll do with it.
My only hope is to please him.

Enter Iago.

IAGO:

What are you doing here?

EMILIA:

Don't be upset. I have something for you.

IAGO:

Something for me?

EMILIA:

What?

IAGO:

To have a foolish wife.

EMILIA:

Oh, is that all? What will you give me in exchange for
This handkerchief?

IAGO:

What handkerchief?

EMILIA:

What handkerchief?
The one Othello first gave to Desdemona,

The one you always asked me to take.

IAGO:

Did you steal it from her?

EMILIA:

No, she dropped it by accident and I happened to be nearby and picked it up.

Look, here it is.

IAGO:

Good girl, give it to me.

EMILIA:

65 What will you do with it?

IAGO:

[Grabbing it.] Why does it matter to you?

EMILIA:

If it's not for an important purpose,

Please, return it to me.

IAGO:

Don't cause a fuss about it.

I need it. Go now.

Emilia exits.

I'll place this handkerchief in Cassio's room,

And allow him to discover it. Little items like these

Become powerful evidence to those who are paranoid.

This may work! Othello is already changing under my influence.

A tiny act can ignite chaos.

Enter Othello.

See, here he comes.

OTHELLO:

Ha! Are you a liar?

IAGO:

What's wrong, Othello? Let's not continue this.

OTHELLO:

Away with you! You've put me in a personal hell.

It's better to be kept in the dark

Rather than know a sliver of truth.

IAGO:

What's the matter, Othello?

OTHELLO:

What reason did I have to suspect her stolen moments of desire?

I didn't see it, I didn't think of it, it didn't hurt me.

I slept soundly the next night, I was carefree and joyful.

I didn't taste Cassio's kisses on her lips.

The person who stays ignorant of theft,

He hasn't lost a thing.

IAGO:

I'm sorry to hear this.

OTHELLO:

66 I would have been fine if the whole army had been with her,

As long as I never found out.

Now, I must say goodbye to peace of mind.

Othello's purpose is lost now!

IAGO:

My lord...

OTHELLO:

Man, make certain that she is unfaithful.

Show me proof. Because if you lie,

It would have been better if you were never born...

IAGO:

Has it come to this?

OTHELLO:

Show me proof without leaving room for any doubts.

If not, your life be damned!

IAGO:

My noble lord...

OTHELLO:

If you spread lies about her and torture me

...nothing worse can be done.

IAGO:

Blessings! O heavens protect me!

Are you a man?

What a twisted world! Pay attention, world...

A straightforward and honest approach is not always the best.

I am grateful for this realization. From now on,

I won't get too close to anyone since love leads to such harm.

OTHELLO:

No, stay.

IAGO:

I should be more practical.

Honesty is a fool's errand, and it often leads to loss.

OTHELLO:

By everything held dear in this world,

I want to believe my wife is faithful,

But I also suspect she is not.

I thought you were honest,

But now I doubt that too.

I need proof. Her reputation is now as ruined

As my own. Be it betrayal or deceit,

I can't bear it. How I wish for clear answers!

IAGO:

I understand, sir,

You are consumed by your emotions.

I regret bringing this upon you.

You seek resolution?

OTHELLO:

Yes, I do, and I insist.

IAGO:

And you may find it, but at what personal cost?

Would you want to witness her infidelity firsthand?

OTHELLO:

Death and damnation! Oh!

IAGO:

This is a tough journey to walk you through.

What can I say then?
Can any proof be satisfying?
Still, if you insist on a direct path to the truth,
Then you can have it.

OTHELLO:

Give me solid evidence that confirms she's been unfaithful.

IAGO:

I don't enjoy this role I'm playing,
But I'm committed to seeing it through.
Cassio is one of these men. While asleep, speaks.
I heard him say, *"Dearest Desdemona,*
Let's be cautious, let's keep our love hidden."
And "*Oh the cruel fate that made you the Moor's wife.*"

OTHELLO:

That's outrageous! Outrageous!

IAGO:

But this is only his dream. It hasn't happened.

OTHELLO:

It suggests a confirmation. Even if it's just a dream, it's
suspicious.

IAGO:

This could add weight.

OTHELLO:

I will rip her apart.

IAGO:

No, stay calm.
She could still be faithful.
But tell me, have you ever seen a handkerchief
With strawberry designs in your wife's possession?

OTHELLO:

Yes, I gifted her one. It was my first gift to her.

IAGO:

I wasn't aware of that.
But such a handkerchief,

I saw Cassio using today to wipe his beard.

OTHELLO:

If that's true...

IAGO:

If that's true, or if he had any of her belongings,

It would make sense with the other pieces of evidence against her.

OTHELLO:

69

Now, I see the truth. Iago, look here:

With this, I demolish all my deep affection. It's gone.

Dark revenge-- come from your shadowy underworld!

Swell, my heart, with your toxic load,

For it is as poisonous as the tongues of snakes!

IAGO:

Relax for now.

OTHELLO:

O, there must be blood, Iago, blood!

IAGO:

Calm yourself, I warn. You might change your mind.

OTHELLO:

Never, Iago. I'm like the Black Sea,

Whose frosty waters are forced to flow.

Now, under the solid sky,

In the proper honor of a serious vow *[He kneels.]*

I promise myself to this cause.

IAGO:

Remain there for a moment. *[He kneels.]*

Othello! I'll follow your orders,

And obedience will bring guilt in me.

They both stand.

OTHELLO:

I acknowledge our pact.

And will immediately put you to the test.

Within three days I want to hear from you

That Cassio is no longer alive.

IAGO:

Your friend will be dead. I'll do it as you asked.

Just let her live.

OTHELLO:

Curse her, unfaithful girl! Oh, curse her, curse her!

Come with me, I need time to plan

A quick end for the beautiful liar.

Now, you're my second-in-command.

IAGO:

I'll serve you till the end.

Exit.

SCENE IV. CYPRUS. BEFORE THE CASTLE

 [Enter Desdemona, Emilia, and Clown.]

DESDEMONA:

Do you know, buddy, where Lieutenant Cassio stays?

CLOWN:

I'm scared to say where he could be.

DESDEMONA:

Why is that?

CLOWN:

He's a soldier. Anyone suggesting a soldier's not truthful is bad

news.

DESDEMONA:

Okay. Where does he stay then?

CLOWN:

If I told you where he stays, I'd reveal secrets.

DESDEMONA:

What are you saying?

CLOWN:

I don't know where he stays.

DESDEMONA:

Can you find him for me based on what you hear?

CLOWN:

I'll ask everyone I know about him and share the answers with you.

DESDEMONA:

Find him and ask him to come here.

CLOWN:

Okay, I'll do it.

Exit.

DESDEMONA:

Where could I have lost that handkerchief, Emilia?

EMILIA:

I don't know, madam.

DESDEMONA:

Honestly, my honorable Moor is very truthful.

And absolutely not like the jealous types, that's my comfort.

EMILIA:

Isn't he jealous?

DESDEMONA:

Who, him? He could never.

EMILIA:

Look, here he comes.

Enter Othello.

DESDEMONA:

72

DESDEMONA:

I won't leave him now until Cassio is called.

How are you feeling, my lord?

OTHELLO:

Well, thank you, my dear. *[Quietly.]*

Oh, it's tough to hide my true feelings.

How are you doing, Desdemona?

DESDEMONA:

I'm doing well, my kind lord.

OTHELLO:

Give me your hand. Your hand feels clammy,

As though you are nervous, my lady.

DESDEMONA:

It's not yet known age or experienced sorrow.

OTHELLO:

This suggests a generous and open heart.

It's a good hand. An honest one.

DESDEMONA:

You might indeed say so.

OTHELLO:

A generous hand.

Old times fought for hearts.

But now we fight for hands, not hearts.

DESDEMONA:

I can't speak of this. Now, about your promise.

OTHELLO:

What promise, my dear?

DESDEMONA:

I have sent to ask Cassio to come and speak with you.

OTHELLO:

I have a tear.

Give me your handkerchief.

DESDEMONA:

Here, my lord.

OTHELLO:

Not this one.

The one I gave you.

DESDEMONA:

I don't have it with me.

OTHELLO:

What?

DESDEMONA:

Truly, I don't, my lord.

OTHELLO:

That's a problem.

That handkerchief was given to my mother by an Egyptian.

She was a seer,

And she could almost read people's minds.

She told my mother that while she kept it,

It would make her lovable and totally win my father's love.

But if she lost it or gave it away, my father's attention...

When she was near death,

She gave it to me and asked me to give it to my future wife.

I did so, and be careful, cherish it like your own precious eyes.

Losing it or giving it away would be a disaster nothing could match.

DESDEMONA:

Could that be possible?

OTHELLO:

It's true. There's magic in its fabric.

DESDEMONA:

Really? Is this true?

OTHELLO:

Absolutely true, so take good care of it.

DESDEMONA:

If only I had it then!

OTHELLO:

Why is that?

DESDEMONA:

Why do you sound so upset?

OTHELLO:

Is it lost? Has it gone? Is it misplaced?

DESDEMONA:

Oh, bless us!

OTHELLO:

What did you say?

DESDEMONA:

It's not lost. But what would you do if it were?

OTHELLO:

What do you mean?

DESDEMONA:

It's not lost!

OTHELLO:

Get it, I want to see it.

DESDEMONA:

I can certainly do that, sir, but I won't right now.

This is a trick to distract me.

Please, let Cassio be accepted back.

OTHELLO:

Bring me the handkerchief! I have a bad feeling.

DESDEMONA:

Now, come on. You won't find a better man.

OTHELLO:

The handkerchief!

DESDEMONA:

Please, let's talk about Cassio.

OTHELLO:

The handkerchief!

DESDEMONA:

74   A MAN who's always

Put his good luck in the faith of your love...

OTHELLO:

The handkerchief!

DESDEMONA:

Truly, you are at fault.

OTHELLO:

Be gone!

Exit.

EMILIA:

Isn't this man acting jealous?

DESDEMONA:

I never saw this before.

Surely there's some magic in this handkerchief,

I'm truly saddened by its loss.

EMILIA:

It doesn't take a year or two to know a man

They consume us greedily, and once they are full,

They burp us out.

Enter Cassio and Iago.

Look, there's Cassio and my husband.

IAGO:

There's no other choice, she must do it,

And, how wonderful! Go and urge her on.

DESDEMONA:

How are you, good Cassio, what news do you bring?

CASSIO:

Madam, I return to my earlier request: I need your help.

I don't want to be delayed.

If my past mistake has hurt him so deeply

Can win back his love,

Then I must accept this for my own good.

And move on to another path,

Accepting what fate offers me.

DESDEMONA:

Oh, kind-hearted Cassio.

I'm not in a position to help right now.

My husband seems a different man.

I barely recognize him.

75 This man I love has tossed my kind words aside!

We must be patient. I'll do what I can for you.

In fact, I'll risk more for you than for myself.

I hope that reassures you.

IAGO:

Is he upset?

EMILIA:

He just left.

IAGO:

Can he be upset?

He must be upset about something serious.

I'll go find out.

DESDEMONA:

I appreciate that, Iago.

Exit Iago.

There must be some important state matters.

It's clouded his usually clear judgement.

In these times, we must remember men aren't gods

And we shouldn't expect them to behave as such.

Oh Emilia, I've been blaming him for his coldness towards me,

But it seems I was wrong to accuse him so quickly.

EMILIA:

Let's hope it is matters of the state, as you think.

And nothing related to jealousy about you.

DESDEMONA:

I've never done anything to make him so distrustful!

EMILIA:

Jealous people don't need a reason.

They are often jealous without one.

But, they are jealous because they are jealous.

It's a hideous feeling that feeds off of itself and intensifies.

DESDEMONA:

I hope God keeps such hideous feelings from Othello's mind!

EMILIA:

My lady, I hope so too.

DESDEMONA:

I will go look for him.

Cassio, wait here.

If I find him in the right mood,

I'll present your case as best as I can.

CASSIO:

I appreciate your help, your ladyship.

Exit Desdemona and Emilia. Enter Bianca.

BIANCA:

Hi, Cassio!

CASSIO:

What brings you out?

How are you, my lovely Bianca?

Honestly, my love, I was on my way to your place.

BIANCA:

And I was on my way to your place, Cassio.

You've been away for a week? Seven days and nights?

Oh, it feels like forever!

CASSIO:

I'm sorry, Bianca.

I've been caught up with other things but I'll make up for the lost time.

Look, Bianca...

He hands her Desdemona's handkerchief.

Can you do something with this?

BIANCA:

Cassio, where did you get this?

This must be from a new girlfriend.

So this is why you've been away! Well, fine then.

CASSIO:

Hold on, Bianca!

Don't jump to conclusions.

BIANCA:

Then where did you get it?

CASSIO:

I don't know. I found it in my room.

It's well made.

77

CASSIO:

I think it would be good if you made a copy of it.

Please do this and give me some space for now.

BIANCA:

Why should I leave you?

CASSIO:

I'm supposed to meet with the general here.

I don't want him to see me with a woman.

BIANCA:

Why not, I beg?

CASSIO:

It's not because I don't love you.

BIANCA:

But you don't show it.

Could we talk later tonight?

CASSIO:

I can only accompany you a little bit, as I have to stay here.

But I promise we'll meet soon.

BIANCA:

That sounds good.

I understand I must wait.

They both exit.

ACT IV

SCENE 1. CYPRUS. BEFORE THE CASTLE

 [Enter Othello and Iago.]

IAGO:

Do you actually believe that?

OTHELLO:

Believe what, Iago?

IAGO:

The kissing in private?

OTHELLO:

A kiss that wasn't approved of?

IAGO:

Or to be alone with her friend in bed for an hour or more,

Without meaning to do anything wrong?

OTHELLO:

Alone in bed with her, Iago,

But not intending to do anything wrong?

This is the devil!

Those who intend to do good,

Yet do that most certainly tempt the devil.

IAGO:

If they do nothing wrong, it's a minor mistake.

But if I give my wife a handkerchief—

OTHELLO:

And what if you do?

IAGO:

Why then, it's hers, sir, and since it's hers,

She can, I guess, give it to any man she chooses.

OTHELLO:

She also needs to preserve her honor.

Can she give that away?

IAGO:

Her honor is something you can't see.

But about the handkerchief—

OTHELLO:

I sincerely wish I'd forgotten about it.

You said he had my handkerchief.

IAGO:

Yes, what of it?

OTHELLO:

That's not a good thing.

IAGO:

What if I had said I saw him doing something to hurt you?

Or bragging about it.

OTHELLO:

Did he say something?

IAGO:

He did, sir, but rest assured,

He won't admit any of it.

79 **OTHELLO:**

What did he say?

IAGO:

Well, he indeed—I'm not sure what he did.

OTHELLO:

What? What?

IAGO:

Lie.

OTHELLO:

With her?

IAGO:

With her, on her, how you want to put it.

OTHELLO:

Lie with her! Lie on her!

Handkerchief—confessions—handkerchief!

It makes me shiver.

Nature wouldn't surround herself

In such dark passion without some instruction.

It's not words that unsettle me like this.

Noses, ears, and lips.

Is it possible?—Confess?—handkerchief?—Oh devil!—

He faints.

IAGO:

Keep working,

This is how naive fools are caught,

And many innocent ladies just like this,

All blameless, face shame. Sir!

Sir, I say! Othello!

Enter Cassio.

What's up, Cassio!

CASSIO:

What's wrong?

IAGO:

Our leader has fallen into a seizure.

This is his second one. He had one yesterday.

CASSIO:

Massage his temples.

IAGO:

Look, he's coming around:
Can you remove yourself for a bit,
He'll recover quickly. Once he's gone,
I would like to discuss something important with you.

Exit Cassio.

How are you doing, boss? Did you hurt your head?
OTHELLO:
Are you making fun of me?
IAGO:
No, not at all.
I wish you would handle your misfortune like a man!
OTHELLO:

80 A MAN who's been cheated on
Is nothing more than a monster and a beast.
IAGO:
Well, then, there are many beasts in a crowded city.
OTHELLO:
Did he confess to it?
IAGO:
Sir, be reasonable.
Remember that any man can be deceived.
Your situation is far from unique.
The devil's favorite trick is to make a man kiss an unfaithful woman.
OTHELLO:
Indeed, you're wise, Iago.
IAGO:
Step back for a moment and be calm.
While you were here, gripped by sadness, Cassio came.
I managed to send him away and made him promise to return and speak to me.
All you need to do is listen carefully to his lies and how he speaks.

I will make him say how he cheated with your wife.
Just watch his reaction carefully.
Be patient and stay in control.
OTHELLO:
Did you hear, Iago?
I will be patient.
IAGO:
Don't rush anything.
Now, will you step aside for a while?

Othello steps aside.

81 Now I have some questions about Bianca for Cassio.
She's a woman who sells herself.
She really likes Cassio,
But just like a lady of the night who deceives many men,
As soon as he hears about her,
He can't help but laugh and joke hysterically.
Here he comes now.

Enter Cassio.

Every time Cassio smiles,
Othello will get more and more suspicious.

To Cassio.

How are you doing, lieutenant?
CASSIO:
I'm worse off.
Thanks to this story you made up. It's hurting me.
IAGO:
Just remain in good terms with Desdemona,
And you'll be fine. *[Speaking lower.]*
If this matter depended on Bianca, how quickly she'd help!
CASSIO:
Oh, poor girl!
OTHELLO:
[Aside.] He's already laughing!
IAGO:

I never saw a woman love a man this much.

CASSIO:

Poor girl, she really does seem to like me.

OTHELLO:

[Aside.] Now he laughs it off.

IAGO:

Can you hear it, Cassio?

OTHELLO:

Now he's insisting for Cassio to tell the story.

Good, that's a good point.

IAGO:

She's spreading the rumor that you're going to marry her.

Is it true?

CASSIO:

Ha, ha, ha!

OTHELLO:

Are you bragging, Cassio?

CASSIO:

Me, marry her? Are you serious?

Show a little respect for my intelligence,

And don't believe such nonsense. Ha, ha, ha!

OTHELLO:

So, so, so. The one who laughs last laughs best.

IAGO:

Honestly, everyone's talking about your alleged marriage to her.

CASSIO:

Is this really true?

IAGO:

If not, then I am a dreadful villain.

OTHELLO:

Have you made a fool of me? Well, well.

CASSIO:

This is her own imaginative thinking. She believes I'll marry her purely out of her love for me and her flattering, but not because of any promise I've made.

OTHELLO:

Iago signals for me. He's starting the story now.

CASSIO:

She was just here. She follows me everywhere. I was chatting with some people from Venice on the sea-bank the other day. She shows up and throws her arms around my neck.

OTHELLO:

Crying, "Oh dear Cassio!" His actions definitely suggest it.

CASSIO:

She clings to me, sobs and pulls at me. Ha, ha, ha!

OTHELLO:

Now he explains how she led him to my room. I see those intentions of yours, but I won't be the one playing into them.

CASSIO:

Well, I need to get away from her.

IAGO:

Look, she's coming this way.

Enter Bianca.

CASSIO:

Here's another troublesome one! Furthermore, a clingy one. Why are you always following me?

BIANCA:

Let evil itself chase you! What did you mean by that handkerchief you gave me earlier? I was a fool to accept it. Am I supposed to do something with it? You found this in your room and don't know who left it? This must be a gift from another girl, and I'm supposed to deal with it? Here, take back your trinket. You can deal with it yourself.

CASSIO:

What's going on, my dear Bianca? What's happening?

OTHELLO:

By the Heavens, that looks just like my handkerchief!

BIANCA:

83

If you'd like to join me for dinner tonight, feel free. If not, come when you feel like it.

Exit.

IAGO:

Go after her, Cassio.

CASSIO:

I have to, or she'll make a scene for all to see.

IAGO:

Are you planning on eating there?

CASSIO:

That's the plan, yes.

IAGO:

Well, I just might stop by because I would really like to talk to you.

CASSIO:

Please do. Will you come?

IAGO:

Enough said; let's not discuss it further.

Exit Cassio.

OTHELLO:

[Stepping forward.] Iago, how should I kill him?

IAGO:

Did you notice how he mocked his misbehavior?

OTHELLO:

Oh, Iago!

IAGO:

Did you see the handkerchief?

OTHELLO:

Was that mine?

IAGO:

Yes, it was yours. Can't you see how he appreciates the silly woman, your wife? She gave it to him, and he has given it to his mistress.

OTHELLO:

I wish I could spend nine years just killing him. She's such a great woman, an attractive woman, a wonderful woman!

IAGO:

No, you need to forget all that.

OTHELLO:

Yes, let her face the consequences tonight. She doesn't deserve to live any longer. My heart has grown cold; when I strike it, it hurts my hand. The world has never seen a sweeter creature. She could be next to an emperor and he'd do what she command.

IAGO:

No, that's not the right approach.

OTHELLO:

Punish her. I'm just saying it as it is. She's so skillful with her needlework, such a fantastic musician! She could soothe the wildness out of a bear! Such intelligence and creativity!

IAGO:

She's made things worse by doing all this.

OTHELLO:

She's messed up so many times, so many times. Yet she's so gentle!

IAGO:

Yes, too gentle.

OTHELLO:

OTHELLO:

No, that's for sure. But it's such a shame, isn't it, Iago! Oh, Iago, it's heartbreaking!

IAGO:

If you're so forgiving of her wrongdoings, let her continue. Because if it doesn't bother you, it doesn't trouble anyone else.

OTHELLO:

I'll cut her into pieces. She dares to cheat on me!

IAGO:

Oh, that's truly a low blow on her part.

OTHELLO:

With my own officer!

IAGO:

That's even worse.

OTHELLO:

Get me some poison, Iago. I need it for tonight. I won't argue with her anymore. Tonight, Iago.

IAGO:

Don't use poison, strangle her in her own bed, the very bed she has dirtied.

OTHELLO:

Good, good. The fairness of it appeals to me. Very good.

IAGO:

As for Cassio, let me be in charge of him. You'll hear more by midnight.

OTHELLO:

Extremely good. *[A trumpet within.]* What is that trumpet sound?

Enter Lodovico, Desdemona and Attendant.

IAGO:

It's something from Venice, definitely. It's Lodovico
He's been sent by the duke. Look, your wife is with him.

LODOVICO:

I greet you, respectable general!

OTHELLO:

And I you, with all my heart, sir.

LODOVICO:

The duke and senators of Venice send their greetings.

Gives him a packet.

OTHELLO:

I accept their regard gratefully.

Opens the packet and reads.

DESDEMONA:

What's the news, dear cousin Lodovico?

IAGO:

I am delighted to see you, sir.

Welcome to Cyprus.

LODOVICO:

I thank you. How is Lieutenant Cassio?

IAGO:

He's alive, sir.

DESDEMONA:

Cousin, there's a misunderstanding between him and my husband. You can help fix it.

OTHELLO:

Are you certain of that?

DESDEMONA:

Yes, my lord?

OTHELLO:

[Reading.] "Be sure to make this happen, or else you will—"

LODOVICO:

He didn't call...

Is there a conflict between my lord and Cassio?

DESDEMONA:

A very unhappy one.

I would do a lot to help them,

considering my affection for Cassio.

OTHELLO:

By fire and fury!

DESDEMONA:

My dear lord?

OTHELLO:

Are you serious?

DESDEMONA:

Wait, is he upset?

LODOVICO:

Maybe the letter upsets him...

As far as I can tell,

they are ordering him home and passing Cassio his powers.

DESDEMONA:

Believe me, I'm glad about this.

OTHELLO:

Really?

DESDEMONA:

My lord?

OTHELLO:

I take pleasure in seeing you upset.

DESDEMONA:

Why, dear Othello?

OTHELLO:

Fiend!

Strikes her.

DESDEMONA:

I don't deserve this.

LODOVICO:

My lord, no one in Venice would believe this.

Even if I swore by that witnessed it: it is too cruel.

Apologize to her. She is crying.

OTHELLO:

Oh monster, monster!

If the earth could sprout from a woman's tears,

Every tear shed by her would be insincere.

Get out of my sight!

DESDEMONA:

I won't stay to offend you further.

She leaves.

LODOVICO:

I urge you, my lord, call her back.

OTHELLO:

Lady!

DESDEMONA:

Yes, my lord?

OTHELLO:

What do you want with her, sir?

LODOVICO:

Me, my lord?

OTHELLO:

Yes, you. You wanted me to make her turn around.

Well, sir, she can turn and turn and keep going,

Turn again. And she can cry, sir, cry.

Carry on with your tears.

About this, sir,

I have been ordered to return home.

I will follow the instructions,

Go away now!

Desdemona leaves.

Cassio will take my place. And, sir, tonight,

I kindly invite you to dine with us.

You are welcome, sir, to Cyprus. Wild and crazy!

He leaves.

LODOVICO:

Can this be the noble Moor?

Who could not be disturbed by emotion?

IAGO:

He has changed a lot.

LODOVICO:

Is his mind still intact? Is he not losing his sanity?

IAGO:

He is as he is. I cannot openly criticize

What he could become. If what he might become isn't,

I wish to heaven it was!

LODOVICO:

What, hit his wife?

IAGO:

Honestly, that was not good. I still wish I knew

That would be the worst to come!

LODOVICO:

Is this his usual behavior?

Or did the letters stir up his emotions,
And newly create this fault?
IAGO:
Such a pity, such a pity!
It would not be honest of me to talk
About what I've seen and known. You should observe him,
And his own actions will show what he is
And I can keep silent: just follow him,
And watch how he continues.
LODOVICO:
I'm sorry that I was fooled by him.

Exit.

SCENE 11. CYPRUS. A ROOM IN THE CASTLE

 [Enter Othello and Emilia.]

OTHELLO:

So you have seen nothing?

EMILIA:

I have seen, heard or suspected nothing.

OTHELLO:

Oh, but you have seen Cassio with her.

EMILIA:

Yes, but I saw no trouble, and I listened

To every word that was exchanged between them.

OTHELLO:

So, they never whispered?

EMILIA:

Not once, my lord.

OTHELLO:

And they never sent you away?

EMILIA:

Never.

OTHELLO:

Not even to fetch her fan, gloves, mask, or anything?

EMILIA:

No, my lord. Never.

OTHELLO:

This is bizarre.

EMILIA:

Risking my reputation, my lord, I'd say she is innocent,

I'm willing to risk my soul.

Let the thought go.

She is the purest woman. If not, no man can be happy.

OTHELLO:

Ask her to come here. Go.

Emilia leaves.

What she says is enough.

She's a keeper of horrible secrets.

And yet, she'll get on her knees and pray.

I have seen her doing it.

Enter Desdemona and Emilia.

DESDEMONA:

My lord, what do you need?

OTHELLO:

Please, my love, come here.

DESDEMONA:

What's your desire?

OTHELLO:

Let me see into your eyes.

Look into my face.

DESDEMONA:

What terrifying thought is this?

OTHELLO:

[To Emilia.] Some of your duties, maid,

Please be alone and close the door.

Cough if anyone arrives.

It's your secret, your secret. Now, go on.

Emilia exits.

DESDEMONA:

What are you suggesting with your words, my lord?

I see anger in your tone, but I don't understand the words.

OTHELLO:

Who are you, then?

DESDEMONA:

I am your wife, my lord. Your true and loyal wife.

OTHELLO:

Prove it.

Swear that you're honest.

DESDEMONA:

Heaven indeed knows that I am.

OTHELLO:

Heaven knows that you are as false as hell.

DESDEMONA:

To whom, my lord? With whom? How have I been disloyal?

OTHELLO:

Oh Desdemona, go away! Go away!

DESDEMONA:

Why are you in such sadness, my lord? Why are you crying?

Am I the cause of these tears?

OTHELLO:

It has pleased heaven to test me with trouble.

Sadly, to make me a lasting figure of ridicule for people to point at,

Slowly and without haste.

I could bear that too, quite well.

But there, what I have in my heart,

Where I either live or not live at all,

The spring from which my feelings flow is drying up.

Be stern, my sweet. Yes, become hardened as stone!

DESDEMONA:

I trust my honorable husband believes me to be truthful.

OTHELLO:

Oh, yes, as the flies are in the butcher's shop,

Their energy revived with each breath of air.

Oh you, a weed, so beautifully fair and with a scent so pleasant,

It hurts the senses to take it in. I wish you were never born!

DESDEMONA:

Oh no, what accident have I made?

OTHELLO:

What sinful act? Dishonor!

You dare to dishonor me in front of everyone!

I could burn with anger and shame if I spoke of your actions.

What sinful act! Shameless woman!

DESDEMONA:

By heaven, you are wronging me.

OTHELLO:

Are you not unfaithful?

DESDEMONA:

If keeping myself pure for my husband means that I am not unfaithful, then I am not.

OTHELLO:

So, not unfaithful?

DESDEMONA:

No, as I hope to be saved.

OTHELLO:

Is this a possibility?

DESDEMONA:

Oh, may heaven forgive us!

OTHELLO:

Then I beg your pardon.

I had mistakenly taken you for that deceitful woman from Venice.

90   This lady who married Othello – you, madam.

Enter Emilia.

You, yes, you!

We've finished here.

Here's payment for your trouble.

Please, lock the door and keep our conversation private.

Exit.

EMILIA:

Oh no, what is this man thinking?

How are you, Madam? How are you, my good lady?

DESDEMONA:

Honestly, I'm exhausted.

EMILIA:

Dear lady, what's wrong with your husband?

DESDEMONA:

With who?

EMILIA:

Well, with your husband, madam.

DESDEMONA:

Who is your lord?

EMILIA:

He who is also your husband, sweet lady.

DESDEMONA:

I have none. Don't talk to me, Emilia.

I can't cry, and I don't have any answer to give you.

But I beg you, tonight dress my bed with my wedding sheets.

Remember, and call your husband here.

EMILIA:

Oh, this is quite a twist!

Exit.

DESDEMONA:

I suppose it's fitting that he treats me this way.

How have I behaved so poorly to deserve even the smallest doubt about my conduct?

Enter Iago and Emilia.

IAGO:

What can I do for you, madam?

How are you coping?

DESDEMONA:

I really can't tell.

People who train young children use gentle methods and easy tasks.

I wouldn't mind if he scolded me like that.

I am not yet used to these kinds of childish scoldings.

IAGO:

Lady, what seems to be the issue?

EMILIA:

Oh dear, Iago.

My lord has said such horrible and heavy things.

DESDEMONA:

Is that how he thinks of me, Iago?

IAGO:

What are you referring to, dear lady?

DESDEMONA:

The things she says my lord claimed I was.

EMILIA:

He labeled her an unfaithful woman.

IAGO:

Why on earth would he?

DESDEMONA:

I have no idea. I'm sure I'm not.

IAGO:

Don't cry, don't cry: oh, what a terrible day!

EMILIA:

Did she really abandon so many noble suitors,

Her father, her country, her friends,

To be called names? Wouldn't that make someone cry?

DESDEMONA:

This is my unfortunate fate.

IAGO:

Curse him for it!

How did this happen to him?

DESDEMONA:

Well, only heaven knows.

EMILIA:

I'd be surprised, some villain,

Some tricky, cheating servant, to gain some advantage,

Didn't devise this story to get him so upset. I'd be surprised if not.

IAGO:

Nonsense, there is no such man. It's impossible.

DESDEMONA:

If any such person exists, let heaven forgive him!

EMILIA:

Forget that! Let hell chew his bones!

Why would he say that? Who's with her?

Where at? What time? What situation? What likelihood?

The Moor's been wronged by some very wicked scoundrel.

IAGO:

Talk quieter.

EMILIA:

Oh, shame on them!

IAGO:

You're being foolish. Off with you.

DESDEMONA:

Oh no, Iago!

What can I do to win back my husband's love?

Good friend, please go to him. By the light of the heavens,

I have no idea how I lost his affections. I kneel here.

His cruel actions can certainly hurt;

And his harshness can ruin my life,

But it will never ruin my love.

I am repulsed now by what he has called me.

IAGO:

Please, just calm down. This is just a phase he's going through.

He's stressed about his work matters,

And is taking it out on you.

DESDEMONA:

If that's all it is—

IAGO:

I promise, that's all it is.

Horns sound from nearby.

Listen to those horns calling us to dinner.

The Venice officials are waiting.

Go inside, and don't cry. Everything will turn out okay.

Exit Desdemona and Emilia. Enter Roderigo.

What's going on, Roderigo?

RODERIGO:

I don't think you've been treating me fairly.

IAGO:

What evidence do you have?

RODERIGO:

Every day you're tricking me with some scheme or plan, Iago. I really can't stand it anymore. I'm not persuaded to quietly accept what I've already foolishly put up with.

93

IAGO:

Will you listen to me, Roderigo?

RODERIGO:

Honestly, I've heard too much already.

IAGO:

You're accusing me quite unfairly.

RODERIGO:

With nothing but the truth.

I've spent all I had.

The jewelry you took from me to give to Desdemona

Could have bribed even the most devoted person.

You said she received them,

And promised me hope and friendship in return,

But I've got nothing.

IAGO:

Alright then, very well.

RODERIGO:

'Very well'? I can't move on, man, and it's not alright.

In fact, I'd say it's pretty bad, and I'm starting to feel like a fool.

IAGO:

Very well.

RODERIGO:

I'm telling you, it's not alright.

I'll make myself known to Desdemona.

If she gives back my jewelry,

I'll drop this whole plan and regret my wrong actions.

If not, be ready for me to seek justice from you.

IAGO:

Well, you've said it now.

RODERIGO:

Yes, and I've said nothing but what I have the full intent of doing.

IAGO:

You know, I see there's some fire in you.

I think slightly better of you than I did before.

Give me your hand, Roderigo.

You have a reasonable complaint against me,

But I've been honest. I promise.

RODERIGO:

There's been no proof of that.

IAGO:

94 Your doubt shows smart judgment. But, Roderigo, if you have what I think you have— which I believe more now than before— things like determination, bravery, and strength—show it tonight. If you don't win Desdemona's love the next night, hold me accountable for my actions and bring about my downfall.

RODERIGO:

Okay, but how? Is it a reasonable and achievable plan?

IAGO:

Well, a special order just came from Venice. The order gives Cassio Othello's job.

RODERIGO:

Really? If that's the case then Othello and Desdemona will come back to Venice.

IAGO:

No, he's moving to Mauritania. He's bringing the lovely Desdemona with him unless an unexpected event happens that keeps them here longer. Nothing can guarantee that as much as getting rid of Cassio.

RODERIGO:

What do you mean by "getting rid of" him?

IAGO:

Well, by making him unfit for Othello's job ...by harm.

RODERIGO:

And that's what you want me to do?

IAGO:

95 Yes, if you have the courage to seize an opportunity for your own advantage. He's dining tonight with a woman of questionable morality, and I intend to join him there. He's unaware of his impending promotion. If you can observe him when he leaves, I'll arrange for it to be between twelve and one, you can act as you wish: I'll be close to support your actions, and he'll be caught between us. Don't be shocked, come with me. I'll provide such a clear justification for his death that you'll feel obligated to carry it out. It's getting late, and the night is slipping away. Let's get to it now.

RODERIGO:

I need more convincing for this plan.

IAGO:

And you will be.

They exit.

SCENE III. CYPRUS. ANOTHER ROOM IN THE CASTLE

 [Enter Othello, Lodovico, Desdemona, Emilia, and their entourage.]

LODOVICO:

Honestly, sir, don't bother anymore.

OTHELLO:

Oh, forgive me. A walk would do me good.

LODOVICO:

Ma'am, goodnight. I sincerely thank you, my lady.

DESDEMONA:

You're always welcome, sir.

OTHELLO:

Would you like to walk, sir?—

Oh, Desdemona,—

DESDEMONA:

Yes, my lord?

OTHELLO:

Go to bed right away, I'll return shortly.

Send away your attendant. Make sure it's done.

DESDEMONA:

As you wish, my lord.

Othello, Lodovico, and their attendants leave.

EMILIA:

How is it going now? He seems nicer than he was.

DESDEMONA:

He said he would return shortly,

and ordered me to go to bed.

He also asked me to send you away.

EMILIA:

Send me away?

DESDEMONA:

Those were his instructions. So, kind Emilia,

Give me my nightdress, and say goodnight.

We don't want to upset him now.

EMILIA:

I wish you had never met him!

DESDEMONA:

I don't feel the same way. I love him so much,

that even his aggressiveness, his warnings, his frown—

Seem kind and endearing to me.

EMILIA:

I've prepared the bed with the sheets you asked for.

DESDEMONA:

It doesn't matter. Honestly, how silly are we!

If I die before you, please, dress my body

With those same sheets.

EMILIA:

Let's not talk of such things.

DESDEMONA:

My mother had a maid named Barbary,

She was in love, and the man she loved went mad.

And he left her alone. She had a song called "Willow",

An old tune, but it told her life's story,

And she passed away singing it. That song tonight

Won't leave my thoughts. I have so much to do,

But all I can think is to drop my head

And sing it just like poor Barbary. Please, hurry.

EMILIA:

Should I get your nightdress for you?

DESDEMONA:

No, help me get undressed here.

This man Lodovico is quite decent.

EMILIA:

A very attractive man indeed.

DESDEMONA:

He speaks eloquently.

EMILIA:

I know a woman in Venice who would have walked barefoot to
Palestine just for a single touch of his lower lip.

DESDEMONA:

Singing.

The poor girl was sighing by a sycamore tree,

    Sing the green willow.

    Her hand on her heart, her head on her knee,

    Sing willow, willow, willow.

    The fresh streams moved past her, echoing her sad cries,

    Sing willow, willow, willow;

    Her tears fell, softening even the stones;

    Leave these here:—

Sings.

Sing willow, willow, willow.

    Please hurry. He'll be here shortly.

Sings.

The green willow must be my headdress.
  No one should blame him, I accept his rejection,—
  No, that's not the right verse.

Listen! Who is that knocking?
EMILIA:
It's just the wind.
DESDEMONA:

Sings.

I named my love false, but what was his response?
  Sing willow, willow, willow:
  If I pursue others, you'll sleep with more men.

Now leave, good night. My eyes are itchy.
Is that a sign of crying?
EMILIA:
It doesn't matter one way or the other.
DESDEMONA:
I've heard as much. Oh, these men, these men!
DESDEMONA:
Do you, in your heart believe that there are actual women
Who would betray their husbands in such a terrible way?
EMILIA:
There are definitely women like that, without a doubt.
DESDEMONA:
Would you ever do such a thing given the chance?
EMILIA
Why, wouldn't you?
DESDEMONA:
Not under any circumstances!
EMILIA:

And I wouldn't either.

Not in the light of day, at least. Maybe if it were dark...

DESDEMONA:

Would you betray your husband for anything? Even the world?

EMILIA:

Well, the world is a tempting offer.

It's a big exchange.

DESDEMONA:

I sincerely think you wouldn't do it.

EMILIA:

Honestly, I think I would, and regret it afterwards.

Of course, I wouldn't do such a thing for gifts.

But for the entire world, who wouldn't turn their husband into a fool to become a queen?

I'd risk punishment for it.

DESDEMONA:

Bless me, but I would never, ever do such a terrible thing.

EMILIA:

Well, a wrong is just a wrong.

And if you have the entire world as your reward, you can easily make it right.

DESDEMONA:

I don't believe there are women like that.

EMILIA:

Oh yes, there are many.

But honestly,

I believe it is their husbands' fault if their wives betray them.

Maybe they aren't fulfilling their duties,

Or wasting our riches elsewhere.

Or they become unreasonably jealous.

They hold us back, or maybe they upset us,

or deprive us of what we once had just out of spite.

Well, we have feelings too.

Although we may hold back to some extent,

99

We can still seek justice.
Husbands should realize that their wives
Have senses just like they do.
We can see, smell, taste both wonderful and terrible things,
The same as our husbands do.
And when our husbands choose to replace us with other women,
Is it just for the thrill? I believe so.
Does love motivate them to do so?
I seem to think that this is the case.
Is it weakness that leads them to betray?
It appears so. And don't we women have our own feelings,
Our own desires for excitement and our own weaknesses,
Just like men do?
If that's the case, then they should treat us well.
Otherwise, they should understand that our wrongdoings
Come from what they do to us.
DESDEMONA:
Good night, good night.
May Heaven help me not extract bad from bad,
but instead improve from the bad.

Exit.

ACT V

SCENE 1. CYPRUS. A STREET

100   *[Enter Iago and Roderigo.]*

IAGO:

Hide behind this large object. He will be here soon.

Hold your sword out ready, strike quickly and deep.

Don't be afraid. I'll be right beside you.

This can make us or ruin us. Think about that,

And make your decision stronger.

RODERIGO:

Stay close in case I mess this up.

IAGO:

Right here beside you. Be brave, and get ready.

He steps away slightly.

RODERIGO:

I don't really want to do this;

But he has given me enough convincing reasons.

It's just a man that will be gone. Come on, my sword; he shall die.

He goes to his position.

IAGO:

I have toyed with his emotions until

He's almost at the breaking point,

And he's getting angry. Now, whether he kills Cassio,

Or Cassio kills him, or they kill each other,

Either way, I profit. If Roderigo lives,

He'll demand I pay back the large quantities

Of gold and jewelry that I have stolen from him,

Gifts I said were for Desdemona.

This cannot happen. If Cassio lives,

He remains a threat and

That makes me look bad. And besides, the Moor

Could reveal me to him... that would put me in serious danger.

No, Cassio must die. Wait, I hear him coming.

Cassio enters.

RODERIGO:

I know his walk-- it's him. You villain, you're going to die!

He rushes toward Cassio.

CASSIO:

That strike would have been deadly,

If my coat didn't protect me better than you knew.

Now, it's my turn to test you.

He draws his sword and wounds Roderigo.

RODERIGO:

Oh, I am hit!

Iago dashes from his position,
injures Cassio in the leg from behind, and leaves.

CASSIO:

I am wounded badly. Help, help! I've been attacked!

Falls. Enter Othello.

OTHELLO:

That's Cassio's voice. Iago has followed through on his promise.

RODERIGO:

Oh, what a villain I am!

OTHELLO:

Yes, that's correct.

CASSIO:

Help, help! I need light! A doctor!

OTHELLO:

It's Cassio. Iago, you've shown bravery and honesty.

You have great understanding of your friend's hardship.

You've shown me that my dear wife is deceitful.

She'll meet her unfortunate destiny soon.

Your stained bed will soon see the consequence of your lust.

Exit. Enter Lodovico and Gratiano.

CASSIO:

Hello there! Isn't anyone on guard duty? An attack has happened!

GRATIANO:

Something terrible must've happened; the shouts are very troubling.

CASSIO:

Help!

LODOVICO:

Listen!

RODERIGO:

Oh, what a villain!

LODOVICO:

It sounds like two or three people groaning.

What a dreadful night.

These could be people pretending to be hurt.

We need to be cautious

About approaching these cries without additional help.

RODERIGO:

Still no one is arriving? I might bleed out here.

Enter Iago with a light.

LODOVICO:

Listen!

GRATIANO:

There's someone, wearing only his shirt,
Carrying a light and weapons.

IAGO:

Who's there? Who's shouting about being attacked?

LODOVICO:

We don't know.

IAGO:

Did you hear someone shouting?

CASSIO:

Right here, please! For the love of heaven, help me!

IAGO:

What's the problem?

GRATIANO:

This looks like Othello's officer, as far as I can tell.

LODOVICO:

Indeed, it's him, a very courageous man.

IAGO:

Why are you all crying so loudly?

CASSIO:

Iago? Oh, I've been badly injured! I need help.

IAGO:

Oh my, lieutenant! Which villains have done this?

CASSIO:

I think one of them is still nearby and couldn't get away.

IAGO:

Oh, these villains!

[To Lodovico and Gratiano.] Do you see them?
Come inside and help.

RODERIGO:

Oh, help me over here!

CASSIO:

That's one of them.

IAGO:

Oh, murderous criminal! You villain!

Stabs Roderigo.

RODERIGO:

Cursed Iago! Monster!

IAGO:

Kill people in the dark, huh?

Where are these violent thieves?

This town is too quiet! Help! I've been attacked!

Who are you people? Are you good or evil?

LODOVICO:

We're as good or bad as you make us out to be.

IAGO:

Signior Lodovico?

LODOVICO:

Yes, it's me.

IAGO:

I apologize for the confusion.

Cassio has been hurt by these villains.

GRATIANO:

Cassio!

IAGO:

How are you holding up, my brother?

CASSIO:

My leg has been split in two.

IAGO:

Oh, may heaven help us!

Get some light, gentlemen. I can bind his wound with my shirt.

Enter Bianca.

BIANCA:

What's going on? Who was calling for help?

IAGO:

Yes, who was it?

BIANCA:

Oh my dear Cassio, my dear, dear Cassio!

IAGO:

Oh, what a surprising twist of fate!

Cassio, do you have any idea who these criminals might be?

CASSIO:

No.

GRATIANO:

I'm sorry to see you like this, I've been looking for you.

IAGO:

Lend me a belt to stop the bleeding.

And, oh, could someone help carry him?

BIANCA:

Oh no, he's fainting! Oh Cassio, Cassio, Cassio!

IAGO:

Gentlemen, I suspect this woman is involved in all this.

What role did you play in this tragedy?

Cassio, stay strong. Let's see.

Can we recognize this face?

My dear friend and countrymen,

Roderigo? I can't believe it. Is this Roderigo?

GRATIANO:

From Venice?

IAGO:

Yes, it's him. Did you know him?

GRATIANO:

Of course, I knew him.

IAGO:

Gratiano, I apologize for my lack of courtesy,

Given these bloody circumstances, I hope you can forgive my manners.

GRATIANO:

It's okay, I'm just glad to see you.

IAGO:

How are you, Cassio? Quick, bring a chair!

GRATIANO:

Roderigo!

IAGO:

Yes, that's him.

A chair is brought in.

Can someone kindly help in moving him,

I'll go and get the general's doctor. *[To Bianca]* And for you, mistress,

Save your strength. The man lying here, Cassio,

Was a dear friend of mine. What provoked this conflict?

CASSIO:

Nothing. I do not even know this man.

IAGO:

[To Bianca.] Why so pale?—Quickly, get him out of here.

Cassio and Roderigo are carried away.

Wait, good sirs.—Are you looking pale, mistress?

Do you see the terror in her eyes?

If you keep staring, more secrets will be revealed.

Look at her. Please, look at her.

Do you see now, gentlemen? Guilt will always make itself known,

Even when people are silent.

Enter Emilia.

EMILIA:

Oh no, what happened? What's the problem, dear husband?

IAGO:

Cassio was attacked in the dark

By Roderigo and his associates.

He's nearly killed, and Roderigo is dead.

EMILIA:

For goodness sake, good Cassio!

IAGO:

This is the result of sinful activities. Please Emilia,

Find out from Cassio where he had his dinner tonight.

Are you trembling at that idea?

BIANCA:

He had dinner at my house, but that doesn't mean I have anything to hide.

IAGO:

Oh, he did? I insist you come with me.

EMILIA:

Shame on you, loose woman!

BIANCA:

I am not a loose woman, I am as honest

As you are, who dare to accuse me like this.

EMILIA:

As me? Hmph! Shame on you!

IAGO:

Dear gentlemen, let's go to see poor Cassio helped.

Come, miss, you'll need to give us more information.

Emilia, hurry yourself to the castle,

And tell the lord and lady what's happened.

Shall we head that way now? *[Whispering]* This is the night

That will either make or break me completely.

Everyone exits.

SCENE 11. CYPRUS. A BEDCHAMBER IN THE CASTLE

 [DESDEMONA IS IN BED, ASLEEP. A LAMP IS BURNING BRIGHTLY. OTHELLO ENTERS.]

OTHELLO:

It's the reason, it's the reason that troubles my soul,
Let me not say it aloud to you, you pure stars!
It's the reason. Yet I won't shed her blood,
Nor harm her fair skin, that's whiter than snow.
Still, she must die, or she'll hurt more men
Let the light go out, and then let her light go out.
Once I extinguish your light,
I wouldn't know how to rekindle your light.
When I have plucked your rose,
I can't make it bloom again,
It must wilt. I'll savor it while it's fresh.

Kissing her.

Oh, sweet breath, you nearly convince
Justice to drop her sword! One more kiss, one more.

Remain like this when you are dead, and I will kill you,
And continue loving you after. One more, and this is the last.

She wakes.

DESDEMONA:

Who's there? Othello?

OTHELLO:

Yes, Desdemona.

DESDEMONA:

Will you come to bed, my lord?

OTHELLO:

Have you prayed tonight, Desdemona?

DESDEMONA:

Yes, my lord.

OTHELLO:

If you remember any sin

You have not yet confessed to heaven and grace,

Ask for forgiveness immediately.

DESDEMONA:

Oh my lord, what do you mean by that?

OTHELLO:

Alright, do that, and be quick about it. I'll wait nearby for you.

I don't want to harm your spirit unprepared,

No, goodness forbid! I would not harm your soul.

DESDEMONA:

Are you talking about harming me?

OTHELLO:

Yes, I am.

DESDEMONA:

Then may heaven show me kindness!

OTHELLO:

Indeed, that's what I wish with all my heart!

DESDEMONA:

If you mean it, I trust you won't harm me.

OTHELLO:

Hmm!

DESDEMONA:

And yet, I'm scared of you, you seem serious

When your eyes flash that way. I don't know why I should be scared,

Since I don't feel guilty, but I am scared nonetheless.

OTHELLO:

Think about your wrongdoings.

DESDEMONA:

They are loves I have for you.

OTHELLO:

Yes, and for that, you must pay the price.

DESDEMONA:

But something is unnatural about paying with your life for loving.

Why are you biting your lip like that?

Some violent emotions are shaking you.

These are signs of something bad, but I still hope, I hope,

They don't mean anything bad for me.

OTHELLO:

Quiet, and stay still!

DESDEMONA:

I will. What's wrong?

OTHELLO:

That handkerchief I cared so much about and gave to you,

You gave it to Cassio.

DESDEMONA:

No, I swear on my life and soul!

Call for him and ask.

OTHELLO:

Dear soul, be careful, beware of lying,

You're heading to your end.

DESDEMONA:

Yes, but I'm not ready to die yet.

OTHELLO:

Yes, soon:

So, admit your wrongdoings freely.

Because denying everything with an oath

Cannot change or deny the strong feeling

That I'm overwhelmed with. You're going to die.

DESDEMONA:

Then, Lord show me kindness!

OTHELLO:

I share that thought.

DESDEMONA:

I swear that I have ever wronged you.

I never loved Cassio more than what honesty allows.

I didn't give him that handkerchief.

OTHELLO:

I swear on my life, I saw my handkerchief in his hand.

I think of it as a sacrifice. I saw the handkerchief.

DESDEMONA:

He must have come across it.

I didn't give it to him. Bring him here to me.

Let him tell you the truth.

OTHELLO:

He admitted it.

DESDEMONA:

What are you saying, my lord?

OTHELLO:

That he took advantage of you.

DESDEMONA:

What?

OTHELLO:

Yes.

DESDEMONA:

He can't say that.

OTHELLO:

No, he can't speak.

Trustworthy Iago saw to that.

DESDEMONA:

My mind is racing! Wait, is he dead?

OTHELLO

If every hair on his head

Were a life, my revenge would end them all.

DESDEMONA:

Oh no, he's been betrayed, and I'm ruined!

OTHELLO:

Enough, you whore! Are you crying for him while I'm here?

DESDEMONA:

Banish me, my lord, but don't kill me!

OTHELLO:

Quiet, you whore!

DESDEMONA:

Kill me tomorrow, just let me live tonight!

OTHELLO:

If you resist—

DESDEMONA:

Just give me a half hour!

OTHELLO:

Once I start, there's no stopping.

DESDEMONA:

Just let me say one prayer!

OTHELLO:

It's too late now.

Smothers her.

EMILIA:

[Within.] My lord, my lord! What's going on, my lord?

OTHELLO:

What's that noise? She's not dead, is she? Not completely?

Even though I'm cruel, I'm also merciful,
I wouldn't want you to suffer.

108 **EMILIA:**

[From outside the door.] My lord, my lord!

OTHELLO:

Who's that?

EMILIA:

[From outside the door.] Good sir, I need to talk to you!

OTHELLO:

Ah, it's Emilia. Wait a moment. My wife is gone.

She's probably here about Cassio.

The noise earlier-- Could she still be alive? Should I let Emilia in? Is that wise?

It looks like my wife is moving; or maybe not.

What should I do?

If Emilia enters, she'll talk to my wife.

My wife? I don't have a wife anymore.

This is impossible to bear! It's a time of great sorrow!

I feel like there should be a huge eclipse now, and that people worldwide should be scared.

EMILIA:

[From outside the door.] Please, let me talk to you, sir!

OTHELLO:

Ah, I'd forgotten about you, Emilia. Come in.

Hold on; I'll open up. Where is she?

Opens the door. Enter Emilia.

What's wrong now?

EMILIA:

There's been a terrible murder, sir!

OTHELLO:

What, just now?

EMILIA:

Yes, sir.

OTHELLO:

It's craziness, like when the moon comes too close to the earth and drives people mad.

EMILIA:

Cassio, sir, has killed a young man from Venice named Roderigo.

OTHELLO:

Roderigo is dead? And Cassio, too?

EMILIA:

No, Cassio isn't dead.

OTHELLO:

Cassio isn't dead! Then everything's off balance, and my plans for revenge are ruined.

DESDEMONA:

Oh, they killed me wrongfully!

EMILIA:

What was that noise?

OTHELLO:

What noise?

EMILIA:

Quickly! That was my dear lady's voice.

Help! Somebody help! Sweet Desdemona, speak again!

DESDEMONA:

I die an innocent death.

EMILIA:

Who has done this?

DESDEMONA:

No one. It was me. Goodbye.

Give my regards to my sweet lord. Farewell!

She dies.

OTHELLO:

Wait, how could she be murdered?

EMILIA:

Sadly, who knows?
OTHELLO:
You heard herself say it wasn't me.
EMILIA:
Yes, she said that. I have to tell the truth.
OTHELLO:
She went off lying, straight to a fiery hell.
It was me who killed her.
EMILIA:
The more of an angel she is,
And you are a dark demon!
OTHELLO:
She became foolish, and she was unfaithful.
EMILIA:
You slander her, and you are a demon.
OTHELLO:
She was as deceitful as the sea.
EMILIA:
You're like a wildfire, saying
That she was disloyal: No, she was truly good!
OTHELLO:
Cassio had wooed her; ask your husband otherwise.
I'd be doomed to the deepest hell,
If my motives for this madness weren't justified.
Your husband was aware of it all.
EMILIA:
My husband?
OTHELLO:
Your husband.
EMILIA:
You're saying she betrayed her marriage?
OTHELLO:
Yes, with Cassio. If she had been faithful,
And if heaven would create another world

Made of one flawless, precious gem,
I wouldn't have traded her for it.
EMILIA:
My husband?
OTHELLO:
Yes, he was the one who first told me.
He's an honest man.
EMILIA:
My husband?
OTHELLO:

110 WHAT MORE REPETITION IS NECESSARY, woman? It was your husband.
EMILIA:
Oh, mistress, deception has played a cruel joke with love!
My husband said that she was untrue?
OTHELLO:
Yes, woman!
I've told you many times!
My ally, your husband, the honest Iago.
EMILIA:
If he insists on that, let his disgusting soul suffer!
He makes up lies.
Her affection was too fierce for her to be a cheater.
OTHELLO:
Ha!
EMILIA:
This action of yours is no closer to earning heaven's grace
Than you were of deserving her.
OTHELLO:
Quiet! It's best you do.
EMILIA:
You don't hold a fraction of the power to cause me harm !
How deceived! How foolish!

As unknowledgeable as dirt! You've committed an act.
And I'll expose you,
Even if it costs me twenty lives. Help! help, ho! help!
The Moor has caused the death of my mistress! Murder, murder!

Enter Montano, Gratiano and Iago.

MONTANO:

What seems to be the problem? What's happening, general?

EMILIA:

Ah, are you here now, Iago?
You have done quite an accomplishment,
You're responsible here.

GRATIANO:

What's the problem?

EMILIA:

Stop this villain, if you're a man.
He claims you informed him that his wife cheated.
I am certain you didn't, you're not that evil.
Speak, as my heart is bursting.

IAGO:

I shared my thoughts to him and that's all.
Then, what he discovered was true for him.

EMILIA:

But did you ever convince him his wife was unfaithful?

IAGO:

Indeed, I did.

EMILIA:

You lied!
A wicked lie!
She's been disloyal with Cassio? Cassio?

IAGO:

Yes, with Cassio, madam. Learn to hold your tongue.

EMILIA:

I won't stay quiet. I must voice the truth.
Our mistress here has been murdered in her bed.

ALL:

Heaven prevent such a tragedy!

EMILIA:

And your tales have put the blame on her.

OTHELLO:

Don't be shocked, everyone. Sadly, it's true.

GRATIANO:

That's an unsettling truth.

MONTANO:

Such a horrifying crime!

EMILIA:

Injustice, injustice, injustice!

It's overwhelming.

In my sorrow, I could end my own life.

Injustice, such injustice!

IAGO:

What, have you lost your senses?

Go home immediately.

EMILIA:

Respectable people, let me say a few words.

I usually should obey him, but maybe not this time.

Maybe, Iago, I won't ever return home.

OTHELLO:

Oh no! Oh no! Oh no!

Huddles over his wife.

EMILIA:

Lie down and weep;

Because you've killed a pure soul.

OTHELLO:

[Getting up.] Oh, she was corrupt!

There's your niece,

Those hands of mine just took away her life.

I understand this action seems monstrous and dreary.

GRATIANO:

Poor Desdemona! It's good that her father isn't living.
Your union brought his end. Had he been living,
This scene would've pushed him to the edge.

OTHELLO:

It's regrettable. But Iago knows
She committed shameful acts with Cassio,
Not once but thousands of times. Cassio admitted it,
And she did reward his romantic efforts.
After all, I saw it in his hand
The handkerchief, an old keepsake
That my father gifted to my mother
Which I had given to Desdemona.

EMILIA:

My God!

IAGO:

Be quiet.

EMILIA:

The truth will come out, it will come out. Silence me?
No, I'll speak freely like a northern breeze.

IAGO:

Be sensible, go home.

EMILIA:

I won't.

Iago tries to stab his wife.

GRATIANO:

Shame on you!
Are you drawing your sword at a woman?

EMILIA:

Oh you foolish man, that handkerchief you're talking about,
I found it by chance and gave it to my husband.
He had begged me to steal it.

IAGO:

Liar!

EMILIA:

Did she give it to Cassio? No, I found it,

And I gave it to my husband.

IAGO:

Liar!

EMILIA:

In the name of heaven, I'm not lying, gentlemen.

Oh, what a dangerous fool! How could such an idiot

Deserve such a good wife?

OTHELLO:

Aren't there rocks in heaven

For something other than thunder?

Something worse?

Iago stabs Emilia and then runs away.

GRATIANO:

You have killed your wife.

EMILIA:

Yes, it's true. Oh, lay me next to my mistress.

GRATIANO:

He's on the run, and his wife's dead.

MONTANO:

He's a well-known villain. Take this weapon

Let's guard the door from the outside, don't let him escape.

I'll follow that wicked man,

For he's truly a cursed servant.

Exit Montano and Gratiano.

OTHELLO:

I'm not brave,

But why should reputation outlive truth?

Let it all go.

EMILIA:

What did your song foretell, lady?

Listen, can you hear me?

[Sings.] Willow, willow, willow...

Moor, she was faithful. She loved you, heartless Moor

As surely as my soul goes to heaven, I speak the truth;
Speaking truth as I believe, I die, I die.
She dies.
OTHELLO:
I have another weapon in this room,
It's a Spanish sword.
Oh, here it is. Uncle, I must come out.
GRATIANO:
[Within.] If you try, it will cost you dearly.
You have no weapon, and must unavoidably suffer.
OTHELLO:
Then come look at me and talk,
Or, unprotected as I am, I will confront you.

Enter Gratiano.

GRATIANO:
What's going on?
OTHELLO:
Look, I have a weapon.
A better one didn't support itself.
I have overcome more obstacles
Than twenty times your attempts to stop me. But, oh empty
brag!
Who can control his own destiny? It's not like that anymore.
Don't be afraid, even though you see me armed.
This is the end of my journey...
And I back away. Where shall Othello go?
What a sight you are now!
As pale as your dress, o luckless lady,
Your tragic appearance will cast my spirit
From the heavens and demons will fight over it.
Freezing, freezing, my dear!
Even as pure as you were.
Cursed, utterly cursed!
Whip me, let the demons take me,

Strip me of this heavenly sight!
Toss me in the wind, roast me in fire,
Cleanse me in the burning depths of a fiery pit!
Oh, Desdemona! Dead, Desdemona! Gone!
Enter Lodovico, Montano, Cassio being carried in a chair, and Officers
with Iago as a prisoner.

LODOVICO:

Where is this unlucky man?

OTHELLO:

That used to be Othello. Here I am now.

LODOVICO:

Where is that snake? Bring the criminal here.

OTHELLO:

I look down towards his feet, although it's just a story.
If you're a devil, I can't kill you.

Wounds Iago.

LODOVICO:

Take his sword away from him.

IAGO:

I bleed, sir, but I'm not dead.

OTHELLO:

I don't feel sorry. I would rather you live.
In my opinion, it's a relief to die.

LODOVICO:

O Othello, you were once so noble, but now you're a criminal.
What should we say to you?

OTHELLO:

Well, whatever you wish. A respectful killer, if you must.
I did nothing from hatred, but all in honor.

LODOVICO:

He has partly admitted his wrongdoing.
Did you conspire with him in Cassio's death?

OTHELLO:

Yes.

CASSIO:

Dear general, I never wronged you.

OTHELLO:

I believe you, and I apologize to you.

115 Why has the devil trapped my mind and body in this way?

IAGO:

Don't ask me anything.

What you already know, you know.

From this time forward, I will be silent.

LODOVICO:

What, not even to pray?

GRATIANO:

Punishment will force you to speak.

OTHELLO:

Well, your way is best.

LODOVICO:

Sir, you need to understand what has happened.

Here's a letter found in the pocket of the deceased Roderigo.

One of them explains the plan for Cassio's death to be carried out by Roderigo.

OTHELLO:

Oh, what a scoundrel!

CASSIO:

Despicable!

LODOVICO:

Now here's another letter.

It appears that Roderigo intended to send this curse to this villain,

But possibly, Iago stopped him.

OTHELLO:

How evil he is!

But how, Cassio, did you come into possession

Of that handkerchief that belonged to my wife?

CASSIO:

I found it in my room.

He just confessed a moment ago that

He dropped it there for a particular reason,

Which served his wicked purpose.

OTHELLO:

What a fool I've been! Fool! Fool!

CASSIO:

Roderigo's letter also reveals how he blames Iago

For setting him against me on watch, leading to my downfall.

And just now, after seeming dead for a long time,

He said that it was Iago who wounded him, Iago who made him do it.

LODOVICO:

You must leave this room and come with us.

You no longer have command here, and Cassio now oversees Cyprus.

As for this villain...

Anyone capable of creating much torment,

He is due to receive. You will be kept as a close prisoner.

Come, let's proceed.

OTHELLO:

Wait. Let me speak a few words before you leave.

I have served the state, and they are well aware of it.

I request you, in your letters,

When you report these regrettable events,

Describe me as I truly am. Do not downplay anything,

Nor write anything in spite or malice. You must speak

Of someone who loved passionately, if not wisely.

Of someone who was not easily jealous, but once provoked,

Became extremely distressed. Of someone who,

Like a common person, carelessly destroyed a precious gem

That was more valuable than all his possessions. Of someone whose tearful eyes,

Though unfamiliar with softer emotions,

Wept forever. Make sure you note this.
And remember to mention that once in Aleppo,
Where a hateful stranger
Abused a Venetian and insulted Venice,
I grabbed that disrespectful man by the throat,
And struck him down, like this.

Stabs himself.

LODOVICO:
What a horrific end!
GRATIANO:
All is ruined by what has happened here.
OTHELLO:
I kissed you before I harmed you.
There's no option left but this,
Ending my own life, to die upon a kiss.

Falls on Desdemona.

CASSIO:
I feared this might happen...
LODOVICO:
[To Iago.] You cruel creature,
More vicious than pain, starvation, or the fierce sea,
Look at the tragic scene you created on this bed.
The object poisons sight,
Let it be hid. Gratiano, keep the house,
And take the fortunes of the Moor,
For they belong to you. To you, lord governor,
Remains the responsibility of this hellish villain.
The time, the place, the torture. Consider this
And punish him.
I'll return to Venice immediately
With heavy heart as a result of these heavy acts.
Keep this hidden. Gratiano. Stay at the house,
And take Othello's property,
For now it belongs to you. For you, honorable governor,

It falls on you to judge this wrongdoer.
The moment, the scene, the agony...
I'll quickly get on a ship, and to the government
With a heavy heart, I'll share this horrible event.

Exit.